I Got a Love Jones

By: Ebony Diamonds

D1527103

Text **LEOSULLIVAN** to 22828 to join our
mailing list!

To submit a manuscript for our review, email us at submissions@leolsullivan.com

© 2016
Published by Leo Sullivan Presents
www.leolsullivan.com

India

"Yeah, nigga, eat this pussy." I moaned as Juelz ate my pussy for the fourth time this week.

I had just started talking to him, and he was already eating the twat and giving me his little Burger King check. I refused to have sex with him, even though I was hitting another guy off anytime I felt the need. I didn't really like Juelz; he was just a mouth to nut in, and that was just fine with me. He was a beast too. He slid his tongue in and out of me like he was slurping on an ice cream cone. I grabbed the back of his head and came hard as he stroked my nipples and lapped up every drop.

"Can you at least give me some pussy this time?" he asked, more like begged.

"No, I'm a virgin. I don't have sex," I said, lying my ass off.

"Lies. This shit not really not gonna work for me then. I need some pussy, I can't just lick you and that's it," he said as he pulled his pants up.

As soon as I got up, my sister, Milan, busted her yellow ass into the room.

"Damn, bitch, you can't knock?" I should have locked the damn door.

"I'm sorry, I just needed a pencil for my math homework."

"Bitch, fuck your homework. Don't you see I'm busy?" I said and threw my cheerleading trophy at the door, trying to hit her.

Milan ducked out and slammed the door. I couldn't stand her ass. She was a straight square, and she just irritated the shit out of me. She stayed under my mother, and I didn't think the shit was cute all. Milan was older than me, so you would expect her to be on some grown shit, but she was just an annoying little mouse who squeaked around.

"Your sister cute as shit," Juelz said as he picked his book bag up.

I went and pushed him, then slapped him in the face.

"Get out! Get the fuck out my house. You want the bitch, go get her," I said and pushed him out the door.

"I'm done with your hoe ass. You ain't fucking anyway."

He was big mad.

"Yeah, I'm fucking, just not you. Now get your dirty ass out my house."

I slammed my bedroom door in his face, then I picked up my phone to text my bae, Brian. He was everything, and I needed some dick after that bomb ass head. Just when he texted me back, my mother barged into the room and she looked furious.

"Who was that who ran out my house just now?" she asked.

Her 5'9" 260-pound frame towered over me. She looked at my legs and saw I wasn't wearing any pants. Before I could blink, she had pulled out a belt and was whooping my ass.

"Ma, stop!" I yelled, grabbing the belt from her. "I'm almost eighteen. I'm a grown woman."

"You're a grown woman? You don't even buy your own toilet paper to wipe your stinking ass. How many bills you pay this month? I can't hear you, India? That's right, not one. If I ever see another one of these lil nappy headed niggas in my house, me and you gonna square up." She backed out the door and slammed it behind her.

I know Milan's ass snitched on me. I'm going to get her ass back too. She was always jealous of me, and I knew why. She hated that I had my father in my life. My father bought me anything I wanted, and he took me on trips whenever I felt like going somewhere. Her father was a deadbeat crack head. My mother had always treated her better for that reason alone.

She was twenty, and in college but she was a straight lame. The one guy she liked, I got him to fuck me. When Milan saw him leaving, I laughed my ass off. She looked so hurt, it was hilarious. Now, she calls herself having a boyfriend that she thinks I don't know about, but her simple ass can't get him to keep his dick in his pants either. Fuck her.

*****

It was dinnertime and my mother wanted us to eat dinner with her like we were a family. I hated the shit because she always force fed me her good girl, good grades bullshit. No matter what grades I pulled, it was still the same thing. She swore I was destined to land on skid row, which was Los Angeles biggest homeless community. They had prostitutes, crack heads, and everything.

She kept comparing me to Milan. *Oh, you should get good grades so you can go to a good college like Milan, or oh Milan is on the dean's list again.* Fucking annoying. She was such a loser ass bitch, she chose not to stay in the dorms so she could be stuck under my mother all fucking day. Ugh.

"Get off your phone, India. You can't talk to us for a minute?" my mother said as she looked at me like she was about to slap me.

"Oh My God. I can't do nothing, huh?" I said and slammed my phone down.

"Ma, I got that nomination from school for my piece in the school newspaper," Milan said with her usual greater than thou attitude.

"That's great, Milan. I'm so proud of you."

I rolled my eyes and slid my plate away.

"I'm going to Channell's house. I'm not really hungry," I said as I backed away from the table.

"You better have your ass in here at ten."

My mother turned her attention back to Milan. I shook my head and went to get in the shower. I was actually going to my boo's house. I grabbed my little pouch with my good Cali bud and got moving. On my way out, I went into Milan's room and took some money out of her drawer. I needed some sheets and something to drink.

When I left the house, Milan was sitting on the couch cracking up while watching Big Bang Theory. *How the fuck is this weak ass bitch my blood?*

I took my beat up ass Honda and drove to Brian's house, stopping at Carl's Jr. on the way. *Thanks, Milan.* I laughed to myself. It would go nice after we got the munchies. When I pulled up, Brian was outside lifting weights. He loved when I watched him do that, even though I really didn't give a shit about it one way or another.

"Hey sexy," he said as he set the weight on the rack.

"Wassup boo." I walked up and kissed him on the lips.

"I missed your ass. Damn, you got a nigga some food?" he said, eyeing the Carl' Jr. bag.

"You know I love to feed you."

I wasn't really talking about food at that point. He smirked because he caught on. We walked inside and his mother and her much younger boyfriend were sitting on the couch smoking.

"Hey, India, look at your cute ass," she said and winked at me.

Her boyfriend, Chance, eyed me, giving me the *fuck me* eyes like he always did. I flirted and played along every chance I could when nobody was watching. He was cute as shit, and she was too old for him, in my eyes anyway. I put an extra switch in my walk when I went by.

We went into the room and ate, and before long, I was getting that good stroke I came for. Call me what you want, but I loved sex, and ever since I was broken in, I just couldn't stop. After we both came, I got up to leave.

"You gonna miss me?" he asked.

"You know I am." I kissed him and backed out the room.

When I closed the door, Chance was standing right behind me. "You lucky she passed out, or she woulda heard y'all." He licked his lips and grabbed his crotch.

"Well, I guess I'm lucky you did, then."

I smirked and walked past him. He stopped me and rubbed my ass, pushing his hands between my legs from the back.

"I know you want me to fuck your little ass," he whispered in my ear.

"No, I know you want me to fuck you. Don't you," I said then blew him a kiss and left out the door.

I laughed at how easily niggas were weak for me. When I pulled off, my phone started ringing and I saw it was Milan.

"What!" I screamed into the phone.

"Did you go in my room?" she asked with that annoying ass Tweetie Bird voice.

"Yeah, so? I needed some money."

"You could have asked me, you know—"

I hung up while she was talking. I wished she'd realize that I didn't give a shit about how she felt about nothing. I turned my music up and bopped my head to the beat and continued enjoying life.

Milan

"I'm so proud of you, Milan," my mother gushed as she handed me an envelope.

I had gotten an apartment with my best friend, Natasha, and I couldn't wait to be on my own again. I was in my junior year at UCLA, and I had moved off campus my sophomore year after somebody kept breaking into my room. Dealing with that was better than dealing with this foolishness in here. Living with my mom was tough because my sister was gonna get me locked up one day for beating her ass. I was never into violence and stuff, but she was pushing my limits. Dismissing the thought of her simple ass, I continued my conversation with my mother. I opened the envelope and it was stuffed with cash. She never ceased to amaze me. I smiled and got up to hug her. Just then, India walked in with her nasty ass attitude.

"Hey, India," my mother said dryly.

"Hey, Ma. I'm going out tonight and I need your car. Mine isn't doing good," she said.

"You must be crazy as hell if you think I'm letting you take my car to go be a hoe. You betta go pump up that 15 speed bike out there," my mother said and turned back to me, disregarding India.

"I bet if it was this whack bitch you would do it," India said as she walked out the room.

My mother started to get up, but she sat back down. I didn't understand her problem with me, but it started after my mother and her father broke up. He would still buy me things when he left and she hated that. She would get mad after I would get accomplishments in school. India had some of her own, but that shit didn't stop her from acting idiotic. She'd turned into a little bitchy teen, and it wasn't cute at all. I didn't pay her any attention because it wasn't worth it.

"So, this should be enough to last you a while right?" my mother said, pulling me out of my own head.

"Yes, Uncle Jess gave me a thousand, and I've been saving my Starbucks checks." I said getting.

I had started working at the Starbucks a few blocks from campus so I could afford to make it on my own. All of my stuff was already at the new place, so I was eager to get into my own space again.

After I kissed my mother, I was gone. I wanted to get a few things from the Target, so I stopped on the way home. Being the considerate person I was, I texted Natasha to see if I needed anything, and she said no. I picked up some cookies, towels, and a new toothbrush to start, but then I saw all of this house stuff and ended up spending almost $300. I loaded my bags after kicking myself in the ass and pulled off.

When I got into the apartment, I quickly dropped the bags and closed the door. Natasha ran out her bedroom room to see what the noise was.

"Damn, I thought somebody broke in this bitch."

Natasha and I had been friends for a few years, and she was closer to me than that demon India. She stood about 5'7" and was on the thicker side, but good thick. She had dread locs, and she always kept them laid. Her personality was a little different than mine. She was more pop offish, and I was reserved. Like when my sister was around and she was talking reckless, Natasha always snapped on her ass, but I really didn't let India get to me. I loved Natasha like a real sister, and she damn sure treated me better than my own.

"These bags almost killed me. I couldn't stop picking stuff up once I started." I picked up the bag and headed to my room with her walking behind me.

"I do that shit all the time in Walmart. A few of us wanted to head out tonight, you wanna come?" she asked, twisting her locs through her fingers.

"I have to study for that damn biology exam, remember? Next time, though." I started to pull my books out so I could knock this homework out before I started studying.

"Okay, I should be doing the same but I can cram. I'm holding you to the next time, heffa," she said and closed my door.

My phone started ringing, and for the hundredth time today, I hung it up. It was Marquise, my now ex-boyfriend. I had caught him at a party in a room with his dick in this stank hoe on campus. He truly thinks I'm overreacting, which is extremely irritating because he would probably do the same thing I was doing. I put my phone on the charger and started to do my homework. I didn't want to give his ass any more of my energy.

I had some text alerts and I knew they were from Marquis. I picked up my phone and saw the messages were still coming through.

POS: Just give me five minutes baby.

POS: Milan…

POS: Just five minutes okay. I can't let some bitch run you away from me.

I rolled my eyes at the text. Some bitch? He stuck his dick in her, so he ran me away. He was making this decision that I had been toiling with all day in my head so much harder. I went to the door and swung it open to catch Natasha just in case she hadn't left yet.

"Tash," I said, knocking on her door.

"Come in, boo."

I opened the door and saw her in the mirror getting ready.

"Can you go with me in the morning? I hate to do this shit then have to go right to class, but I need it done." It hurt to even talk about it so casually.

"I got you, sis." She walked over, hugged me, and went back to getting dressed.

I went back in my room and tried to finish my homework, but my abortion was the only thing on my mind now.

*****

I was a nervous wreck the next day. I went to class as usual, but I had some time before the abortion, so I went to the grassy area people usually used to chill and sit around. I picked a spot and pulled out my books. Maybe I could get some studying done. I was only about 15 minutes in when Natasha walked over to me and flopped down in the grass.

"I swear that bitch is irritating, Milan."

"Professor Manwon in your butt again?" I asked.

"Ass, Milan, you can say ass, you grown. Jesus," she said and pushed me.

People always made fun of my "clean" mouth and shy behavior. I cursed in my head a lot, but never out loud.

"Damn, if he wasn't my friend cousin, baaaaby," she said, looking toward the group of guys walking past.

I knew exactly who she was talking about. Cain.

Cain was the star quarterback on the football team at school. He also had a reputation for smashing a lot of girls and a few other things. I heard a few people saying he was where you went if you wanted to get certain stuff; I guess they were talking about drugs. I didn't really deal with people like that, but I couldn't judge him. He was too cute, and apparently smart, since I heard he was pre-med, to be doing something stupid like that. I wasn't asking around. It was just what I heard.

"Hey, Cain," Natasha called out.

"Wats good, shawty?" He approached us looking God like. "How you doin' Ms. Lady."

He smiled and I almost wanted to kiss him on those beautiful pink lips. I could tell he took pride in his appearance. He had to be about 6'7" and a good 300 pounds, and he always looked good.

"Oh my God." I accidently said out loud.

"You aight?" He laughed and leaned down like he was checking on me.

"I'm Milan," I said, feeling completely embarrassed.

"I'm Cain, nice to meet you, sweetheart." He winked.

"Aye, you can grab that shit from Craps," he said and pointed at Natasha.

She nodded and we both watched him walk away.

"Lord, that boy fine, girl. You see that beard? I'm a sucka for it," Natasha said and shook her head.

"Yeah, I guess," I said and looked back into my book.

"Girl, you fakin' like shit. I heard you speak ya mind. Oh my God." She mimicked me.

"Oh shut up. What you supposed to be getting?" I asked.

"Some smoke, girl. What you think? He the plug, boo," she said as she took out her phone and looked at it.

He was interesting.

India

I swear I couldn't wait until this week was over and I graduated Saturday. I guess my grades were nothing to really write home about, but it would work, and my GPA was just good enough to get into most schools. I planned to go to UCLA where Milan went. I got accepted, but I didn't tell my mother or her. They wouldn't have given a fuck anyway. It's always been like that. I guess that's why I was how I was.

I was in 7th grade, and I had just found out I won the last slot in the academic bowl for our school. I was so excited that I ran all the way home to tell my mother. When I got home, my mother was sitting on the couch watching TV. I gave her the paper.

She clapped her hands and gave me a big hug. "I'm so proud of you, India. We can go eat wherever you want tonight," she said.

"Okay, I'm about to go change." I ran off to my room and grabbed a pair of jeans and a pink crop top. I took some pictures and posted them on Facebook. Then, I heard my mother screaming at the top of her lungs. I ran out to see what was going on.

"Can you believe it?" Milan asked, jumping up and down.

"India, I got invited to eat dinner with the mayor tonight because of my perfect grades since elementary." She smiled.

"That's good, Milan, but guess what? I'm gonna—"

"Hold up, India. So how many people can go?" my mother asked Milan, completely cutting me off.

"Only two." She set her book bag down.

"You should be okay until we get back. Right, India?" my mother asked me.

I was hurt because she had completely forgotten about what she said we were going to do.

"I thought we were going out." I was getting mad now.

"We can do it tomorrow. We'll be back."

She got up and ran to her room. I could hear her saying how they needed to find new dresses and everything. That was the night I realized the only person who mattered was my sister. No matter how many good grades I had, nobody cared. I started to change because I felt that being good was bad. Well, for me anyway.

I tapped my pencil on the desk while I was being ear fucked by my history teacher about final class projects, and I couldn't care less. I would get the same fool who did all my big assignments to do it. I had promised him a kiss, and he'd been holding onto it for the last two years. Dumb ass nigga.

It was Friday, and I was ready to get the hell outta there so I could get fucked up and bang with my woes. I had two best friends; one was Kitty, and the other was Channell. We had been cooling since the ninth grade, and I wouldn't trade them bitches in for the world. They were more like sisters to me than Milan was, and that was cool with me. It tickled me when Milan moved out, I guess she was tired of getting punked by her little sister.

The bell rang and we were finally free! Channell was talking to her boyfriend by the locker, and I went up to interrupt.

"Bitch, come on," I said, looking at Juelz with a smirk on my face.

Yes, Juelz was her boyfriend, and call me what you want, but she would do the same to me if she had the chance. Doesn't mean I didn't love her.

"Okay, you don't see me talking?" She kissed Juelz on the same lips he had been eating my pussy with, then we walked off and went to Kitty's locker.

"Look at my favorite pussy," I said, making a joke about her nick name.

"Hey hoes, what y'all 'bout ta do?" she asked as she did our secret handshake with each of us.

"Nothing. Ready to get some real food instead of this prison shit they serving."

"That's a bet. I can go for some Fat Burger," Kitty said.

"Nah, let's go to that Burrito spot off the boulevard, that shit bomb," Channell said, rubbing her hands together as she thought about the food.

"Yeah, I like they food. Let's do the mufucka."

As I was walking out, I saw my ex-boyfriend Darren sitting on his car talking to his new girlfriend. I decided to be a little bitch and walk over there. My bitches followed suit.

"Aaaaw, look at the love bugs," I said slowly as I clapped my hands.

"Aye, go 'head with that bullshit, India." Darren said and pulled La'Rhonda closer to him.

"Ain't no bullshit. I just wanted to let you know the shit you gave me finally cleared up. Did yours?"

La'Rhonda looked down to his crotch, and we all started snickering while we walked off.

"You so mean," Kitty said.

"Girl, fuck him and that lopsided bitch." I said and flipped my tracks back.

"You act you he ain't catch you with Brian's ass boo loving and shit. Give him a break, hoe."

"Girl, once mine, always mine."

I went in my phone to text my father about getting some new clothes. He texted me right back that he would put some money in my bank account. My father was Marshall Saunders. He used to play for the Oakland Raiders, and that's how he met my mother. She was a personal trainer for them before we moved to L.A. He had dough for days, and since I knew that, I was getting all the coin I could handle.

I got in my car, which I was going to ask my father to upgrade, and pulled off. When we got down the boulevard, I knew I had to be tripping. I saw Milan and her over done ass friend going into the abortion clinic. Oh, this was too good to be true. I knew it wasn't Natasha because she didn't have the terrified look on her face. It was Milan's ass.

I bucked a U turn and parked in front of the clinic.

"What the hell we doing here?" Channell asked, looking at the building.

"I just saw Milan go in here. I finally got something on her goody two shoes ass."

They both laughed and got out the car. I opened the door with my phone ready and hit the *Live* button on my Facebook. Milan was signing in, so I knew it was her for sure.

"Say hi to Facebook, big sis!"

When she saw me standing there, she looked like she had seen a ghost.

"India, what the hell you doing?" she asked while I still had the video recording.

I went around the clinic and started to narrate.

"Look at my perfect big sister coming in the clinic to get scraped," I said as I laughed.

Her friend Natasha got up and pushed the phone out my hand. "You might scare her, but I will fuck your lil' ass up in here. Take your busted ass goons and turn around," she said, standing directly in my face.

"Yeah, whatever. Have fun, big sis," I said and walked out with my friends.

I finally had one up on that bitch. I'd never had an abortion, and I couldn't wait to tell my mother about her favorite daughter.

We ate quickly and went back to school. I couldn't wait to tell my mother what I had seen today when I got home. When I got there, she was crying and on the phone with someone who was clearly saying something to upset her.

"It's okay, baby. I'm not mad at you. I love you, okay?" she said into the phone and then hung up.

"Who was that?" I asked with my arms folded.

"Your sister. Poor thing had an abortion today, and she was scared to tell me."

Ugh! I hated her, she always takes everything away from me.

"I guess your little angel ain't perfect as you thought, huh?" I said, gritting and walking toward my room.

"You irk my soul sometimes!" I heard my mother scream when I entered my room.

I lay back on the bed, mad because I wanted to bust her ass out, but I guess she thought it would be okay to just say something herself. I couldn't stand her. I looked at my phone and saw I had a bunch of text messages. Of course, Channell and Kitty wanted to know if I screamed on Milan to my mother, but I told them she beat me to it. The next was from Juelz. He wanted to come over. I laughed because this was the same clown who said he was done with me. I might see what that dick do tonight, though.

I texted him back saying he could come, and that I wanted my pussy licked until I was satisfied, and then I would give him some for the first time. He agreed and sped right over. Simple ass niggas.

Milan

I honestly never thought she would stoop so low, but this bitch has truly gone too far. I should have knocked her teeth out her mouth, but I've never been violent that way. I knew she was going to run home to tell my mother, so I beat her to it. My mother was so understanding, and she never even judged me for it; I loved her for that.

Marquis had stopped calling, so I guess he got the point. I was happy I decided not to carry out the pregnancy because he was no good for me anyway. I had seen him on campus later that day, and as soon as he locked eyes with me, he started to jog over. Hell no. I cut through a hall and went into the women's bathroom. I know it sounds like a little much, but I didn't want to see him.

Lying in my bed crying had my eyes puffy as hell, and it looked terrible. I heard banging on the door. It scared me because I was alone in the apartment. Not knowing what to do, I grabbed the hammer that I was using to nail my pictures up just in case I had to bash somebody in the head. I went to the door and looked through the peephole to see that Marquis was standing on the other side. I didn't think he would come there. I had given him the address to our place before we broke up.

"I know you in there, bae," he said as he banged on the door.

"I'm not your bae, baby, boo, honey, I'm nothing to you. So, please leave," I said and leaned against the door.

"No, I think we really need to talk. What's this shit about a Facebook post? You went to the clinic!" he yelled.

I squeezed my eyes closed and turned around, swinging the door open. He was screaming loud enough for my neighbors to hear. He rushed inside before I could even invite him in.

"Look at your face. You been crying?" he asked.

"What the hell do you care?"

"I love you, so why wouldn't I care?"

"What did you want again?" I asked like I didn't remember. I just wanted to stop his ass from trying to sweet talk me.

"Why were you in the abortion clinic? You sister posted a video of you signing in."

"I hate her so much. She took it down, but I'm sure enough people saw it," I said then went to the couch and sat down.

"So, you did have an abortion."

"Yeah, okay? Dag"

"Why did you do that to me, Milan. You didn't even give me a choice in this shit. You killed my baby and didn't even tell me. Well, was it mine? Because that's the only reason I could think of for you to keep some shit like that from me."

I bucked my eyes, not believing what the hell he was saying to me.

"Of course it was yours! Unlike you, I know what it means to be faithful," I said with tears forming in my eyes.

"I can forgive you if you can forgive me. I fucked up bad, and I know it ain't shit I can say to get you to see how sorry I am. I was drunk, and shit just happened."

"So, you do that every time you drink? Why would I come back to somebody like that, Marquise?" I didn't understand his logic.

"Because I love you, Milan. I promise you it will never happen again, just let me stay the night and we can talk." He grabbed my hand, and for a minute I thought about it, but I quickly came back to my senses.

"Bye, Marquise. I might be what people call nerdy or whatever, but I'm not that green to where I don't see bullshit. Go find your hoe and be happy."

I got up and opened the door for him as he walked out. He started to turn toward me, but I slammed the door. He really thought I was a fool.

Of course, the rest of the night, he sent me texts declaring his undying love, but I ignored it.

****

I hated that my mother wanted me to go to this graduation, but I had agreed so she could leave me alone about it. I was still upset about what India did, and I couldn't care less if she graduated. Refusing to put any effort into my look, I put on some jeans and a boyfriend tee after lotioning my body up. Then, I sprayed on my Halle Berry and added lip gloss. I looked so plain.

After I grabbed my purse, I left out the door. I was hungry, so I decided to stop at Dunkin Donuts before I headed to Mom's house. I ordered my donuts and a mocha. She handed me the donuts, but said I would have to wait for the coffee. I bit one of the donuts and accidently broke it in half, so I looked like a dog with a bone in its mouth.

"I'm seeing you a lot more lately," I heard a voice beside me say.

I looked over and saw Cain laughing. "Hungry, huh?"

I realized I still had the donut in my mouth. He must have thought I was awkward as hell by now.

"Your coffee." The lady pushed my cup to me.

My face flushed in embarrassment, and I didn't even say anything to him. I started to walk off and he came up and stopped me.

"Why you running of?" he asked, pushing his hands into his sweat pants pockets.

"I'm not, I just gotta go."

I said stepping back and fell on my ass. Some girls started laughing and Cain looked at them.

"Shut the fuck up!" he barked.

Cain grabbed my hand and helped me up. I had wasted coffee all on my shirt.

"You okay, Milan, isn't it?" he asked.

I can't believe he remembered my name.

"Yes, and yes. I should just get going." I was so embarrassed.

"Girl, get your ass over here," he demanded while he pulled some napkins out the dispenser.

As he wiped my face and my chest, he smelled so good, I just stared at his lips. I swear I think I leaned in to kiss him.

"You all good now," he said and slammed his hand on the counter. "Get her a dozen of whatever she wants and some more coffee. Oh, and gimme my shit too," he told the lady.

"Thank you," I said, kind of blushing.

"It's nothing, beautiful. See you around, aight?" He left and I was zoned out until the lady got my attention.

I grabbed the donuts and coffee then left. I had to hurry home to change. At my apartment, I got in and out within un minutes, then went straight to Mom's house, eating donuts the whole way. When I got there, I went in and saw my mother taking pictures of India in her cap and gown.

When India looked at me, she rolled her eyes.

"Hey, ma. I'm sorry I'm late. I burned myself with coffee in Dunkin Donuts and had to go change," I said.

"Aaaw, you okay, honey?" she said, coming over to look at me.

"She grown. Why you always gotta find a way to make every day about you?" India said as she snatched her purse off the coffee table.

"I wish you'd shut up sometimes, India. That crybaby stuff is annoying as hell."

I rolled my eyes at her and she put up her middle finger.

"Cut the shit. Let's go," my mother yelled.

We got into my mother's Expedition and rode off. The ceremony was shorter than I thought, thank God. I was ready to go. I declined dinner because I didn't want to be around India at all. I asked my mother to drop me off before she went to eat.

When I got to my car, I hurried home so I could do some more homework before I went out with Natasha and our friends.

*****

"Yaaaaaaaas, look at you, Milan," Natasha said as she checked out my dress for the night.

It wasn't really my style, but she'd insisted I buy it and wear it. It was a tight-fitting leopard print mini skirt. The top was sewn into the skirt and was split down to my navel. I felt so out of pocket. I put my hair into a bun and put on some red earrings she gave me. I could barely walk in those damn heels, but I was okay for the most part. My face looked flawless; all I had to add was eyeliner and mascara. I didn't do a lot of makeup, but when I did, it made me look even better.

I opened my bedroom door, and when I entered the living room, I saw our friend Mariah, her sister Janay, and their cousin, Cain. Why was he here? I couldn't stop looking at him, though. His athletic build along with his chocolate skin made my heart skip a beat. I was nothing like the always perfect, always made up, big butt females at school, so I doubted I had a chance with him. Truthfully, after Marquise, I didn't think I was ready to date. I didn't miss the lustful look that Cain gave me as I spoke to everyone, but I ignored it.

"Everybody ready to go?" Natasha asked.

I liked her outfit. She had on a cute red romper, and a pair of tall platform cheetah print heels.

"Let's smoke before we roll. I got some Arbor Mist," Mariah said.

Cain sucked his teeth "I ain't drinkin' no fuckin' wine, y'all can keep that female shit," he said and pulled out a bottle of V.S.O.P. then cracked it open.

I didn't really do hard liquor, so I drank some of the wine. It was good. I wanted it to help me chill a little bit, and it did that. Natasha, Mariah, and Janay smoked, and Cain and I just sat there looking at each other and smiling. He winked at me and my heart dropped. He was sexy.

They finished up, and we all left out the apartment and hopped into Mariah's Jeep. We listened to music the whole ride, and I would have kept riding all night if I had a choice. I was sitting in the back next to Cain and Natasha. Cain was on my left and I could smell his cologne like he'd just put it on. I could feel him looking over at me as we drove, and it made me bite my lip from nervousness.

"You look good as a shit, shawty," Cain whispered in my ear. Jesus, he smelled so good.

"Thank you." I blushed.

"You got a man?" he asked, looking at my thighs and tracing back up to my face.

"I did," I said.

I could feel his eyes on me.

"That nigga must be stupid," he said and looked forward.

When we arrived at the club, it was packed. We even had to stand in the VIP line for ten minutes. When we finally got inside the club, all of the girls immediately started dancing with each other, while Cain stood back and watched. I noticed a lot of girls coming around him and trying to be in is face, but he was ignoring them. He was standing closest to me, and though he spoke to a few people he knew, he hadn't left our group.

By the third song, I was having a ball and glad that I had come out. I was loving Rhianna's *Sex with Me* that was playing. I didn't notice Marquis until he was all up on me.

"So, you out here with that nigga Cain, huh?"

"Huh? We all came together," I said and shrugged.

Marquise shook his head and looked me up and down. "You just had an abortion and you in here poppin' your pussy for all these niggas already. So much for your good girl shit."

I reared back and slapped the shit out of him. He held onto his face and looked at me angrily.

"I think you better get out of my face." I couldn't believe that he was talking to me like he had lost his mind.

"That probably wasn't even my baby." Marquis shot me a hateful look and walked off.

I was determined not to let his ignorant ass ruin my night, but when I looked up and saw who'd come to the party, my mood was more than ruined. India's bitch ass was there, and she was all up in Cain's face. Since she knows none of my friends like her, she pulled Cain off to the side and placed her hand on his chest as she whispered in his ear.

That fucking bitch was like a fly. I couldn't get rid of her ass.

Cain

I was jolted out of my sleep by my alarm, which sounded at 5:00 A.M. every day. Being on the football team, I had to make sure my body stayed right, so I ran 10K every morning before I went to class. I was still tired from the night before and didn't feel like doing shit. I ended up leaving the club so I could start breaking down bricks. I was tired as shit, and barely got two hours of sleep. I couldn't get Milan and how good she looked out of my mind the whole night we were out until her sister came and wrapped me up.

I gave her my number and she texted me to save hers. She let it be known all night how much she didn't like Milan. She told me she was a thirst trap and she'd had so many abortions that she couldn't have kids anymore. I was shocked and skeptical of the that because I'd heard nothing but good things from my cousins. I didn't really take what she said to heart because I always wanted to get to know somebody myself. I had to hold bitches I fucked with to a high standard because of the reputation I'd built for myself out here.

I wasn't your regular ass college nigga, either. I flipped more bricks than a mason. An educated thug, I guess you could say. I didn't want to do this shit forever, though. Once I get drafted this shit was done. I wasn't no type of kingpin, but I had a certain amount of respect out there.

I stood up and stretched, adjusting my dick in my boxers before grabbing my running gear and getting dressed. After making sure my breath was fresh, I grabbed my water and was ready to go. Once I had my headphones in, I started my music and walked out my apartment to warm up.

I started my run, and no sooner had I started, I saw Milan coming out of her building fumbling around with a bunch of books and a few bags. We lived in the same off campus complex, so I saw her quite often. When Mariah had suggested that we go out with her and her roommate, I was down with it. She dropped her books and I ran over to help.

"What's good, Milan?" I said, reaching down and grabbing her books for her.

"Hi, Cain. Damn, it's early to be running," she said with that pretty smile she always wore.

Shawty was a nice ass piece.

"I know, but you out here, so what's your excuse?" I licked my lips as I looked her up and down.

"I have to finish this paper before my first class. Since my laptop clunked out, I have to go to Fed Ex Kinkos."

"Oh, okay. Well, be safe, aight."

"I will."

She smiled and walked away to get in her car. I was about to continue my run when I saw a bottle of pills that she must have dropped out of her bag. I picked them up and couldn't help but notice what it was. Methagine. Since I was pre-med, I knew exactly what those pills were for. Abortionists gave them to broads for bleeding. Wow. I can't believe India was telling the truth. That made me look at her a little differently, but since it was her body, I had to respect what she did with it. I could just never deal with a woman who keeps getting abortions because she's been fucking raw with so many dudes. It just wasn't attractive, and the shit was trifling as fuck.

"Aye, you dropped your pills," I said, walking up with my hand extended.

"Oh, thanks." She grabbed the pills and pushed them back into her purse.

I ran off and continued my run. Damn, she seemed too perfect anyway.

*****

A few days later, I watched my coach as he sat in his office chair with a huge grin across his face. He was holding a letter from the New England Patriots. As he read, I still couldn't believe my ears. They wanted me to come practice with the team to see if I could fit in with them. I mean, I was putting up numbers as a young college QB, but this was professional ball.

"I told you. I knew you would make it, Wilson," he said and handed me the letter.

"This shit seems unreal, coach," I said as I read over the letter.

"It is real, Cain. You're going to kill them dead. Now go to whatever it is your kids do when you celebrate. Turn up, right?"

I busted out laughing because his old ass swore he was down.

"Aight, Coach."

"Oh, Cain, you got a lil something?" he asked and pointed at his nose.

I went in my pocket and pulled out the two grams I had vialed up for him. He was a serious cokehead, but you couldn't say the nigga didn't handle his shit.

I walked out the office with a huge grin on my face. When I called my father to let him know what was up, he wasn't happy like I thought he would be. He was a Dallas fan since we were from Texas, so that's who he thought I should play for. I wasn't about to let him fuck my head up. What he really wanted was for me to keep up the family empire and push weight, but fuck that. I was about to do what I always wanted to do. Play ball.

After getting off the phone with him, there were two text messages in the window. I scrolled down and smiled.

India: Gm.

Attached was a picture of her smiling. This was the first time I'd talked to her since we met, so I decided to call her. I needed to celebrate tonight, and I could use a cute joint on my arm.

"Hey, Cain," she said in a little voice.

I knew he was trying to be cute and shit.

"Wassup, you wanna fuck with me tonight?"

"I sure do. It's my birthday, I just turned eighteen."

"Oh damn, happy birthday, shawty."

I wish the fuck I knew her ass was 17, I'm glad I ain't do shit with her yet. What the fuck was she doing in a club?

"Thank you, Cain. So, I'm down. You going to pick me up?"

"Yeah, I got you. Text me your address."

I pulled out a blunt and smoked on the way home. I wasn't worried about drug test. My coach always got me some clean piss so he could keep getting this raw shit I hand him.

After we hung up, I went to my apartment and got showered and found something to throw on. I decided on my new Versace T-shirt, a pair of khaki shorts, and loafers. I was a fan of watches, so I found my big face diamond encrusted Invictus watch and trapped it on. I grabbed my ear studs and put them in my ears, then I checked my self over in the mirror, I fucked with the gentleman look I had going on. I was ready.

I sent a text to India to let her know I was on the way. When I started to drive through the parking lot, I saw Milan with a pair of shorts and a tank top on. She looked good in even the basic shit. She smiled and waved. I just nodded. She looked confused that I didn't smile and stop, but I couldn't entertain a bitch like that.

India

I was overly excited for my date with Cain's big sexy ass. I had canceled my dinner with Brian so I could go with him. He was upset, but he would get over it. I sprayed some Gucci perfume on and confirmed that I was the shit and ready to go. I had on a blue fitted jumper and a pair of blue and white high top Jordans. I wasn't extremely girly, and I loved tennis shoes. It looked right, though, so I was rocking with it. I decided to wait outside on the porch so that I wouldn't have to be in the house a moment longer.

My mother had told me that Milan was on the way so they could go to the movies. I wish she'd get a damn life. That's her Saturday night, going to the movies with her mother. I didn't feel like being around her ass since she was still salty about that Facebook shit. She could come with it if she wants to, and that bitch Natasha won't be here to save her. They probably fucking. I wouldn't be surprised.

I walked out into the living room and my mother was on the phone with one of her friends talking about people. It's always the busted ones that got the most to say, and that was my mother's friend Juicy. I was sure that was her on the other end. She looked like the friend who was with Robin's ex-wife on BeBe's kids.

"I'm gone, Ma. I'm about to go sit on the porch until my friend gets here."

She looked me up and down and pressed the phone to her chest so that the other person couldn't hear.

"You better bring your ass in here at a decent time too, India."

"Ma, I'm grown now. I don't have to be in by the time the street slights come on no more," I said and laughed.

"Yeah, try me, and you gon' end up on skid row." She put the phone back up to her ear and started cackling again.

I walked outside and sat on the porch to wait for Cain. I had gotten a text from Juelz asking to see me. I laughed and didn't even bother to text him back. I thought he was being too clingy now, and he was going to get us caught. Channell and I went back and forth with texts until I saw headlights then a Mercedes pull up. It was clean, and I prayed it was Cain.

I saw the car light up in the inside because the driver door opened. It was him. Putting on a huge smile, I started walking down the steps. Damn, he looked good when he walked around the car to greet me. He was huge.

"Damn, look at you. Them tennis shoes a nice touch," he said as he walked up and kissed my cheek.

"Thank you." I smiled like a fool.

"No thanks needed, shawty. Let's get out of here."

He opened the car door, and just when I was getting in, Milan pulled up right behind Cain. When she got out, it looked like she got punched in the gut when she saw me with him.

"Hey, Cain."

She smiled at him and walked past me gritting. I rolled my eyes and got in the car. Milan looked back at us, and she was mad as shit from what I could see on her face. I brushed her off and we headed out for our night.

The drive was pleasant enough. He wasn't really talking about much except for football, which I really wasn't interested in. That was until he told me that some NFL team was looking to sign him. This could be my big chance. I had to play my role and make this nigga fall for my ass, and fall hard. I could see myself as a famous football star's wife. Shit, I could probably get a TV show or some shit. Oh yeah, I was going all in.

We had dinner at a very nice restaurant in Hollywood Hills called Che' Olay. It was an Italian restaurant, and it was really fancy. I had never been anywhere like this before. When we walked in, they treated us like royalty. I didn't know what it was, but he had much respect. We sat at the table talking and laughing, and I was truly giving him my best good girl routine. I had explained my plans to go to school for pre-med after I saw his student ID hanging from the rearview mirror. I kind of kicked myself because now I had to really major in the shit when I went to school.

He sat across from me smiling and talking about the major we now shared. That was step one, have something in common. Shit, if he didn't make it in the NFL, he could still be a doctor. I would still be set. He was certainly a keeper.

"Do you want to come chill at my place for a while?" he asked as he signed the check.

"I don't know, I'm not the type of girl who just sleeps around, and especially not on a first date."

"I wasn't asking you to sleep with me. I asked if you wanted to chill."

"I'm just saying. If you think I'm just some hoe, you can just take me home."

This was all a part of my plan. Play the shy, 'I don't sleep with anybody' role, and he would respect me more and see me as wifey material.

"Man, shut that shit up. You know damn well you don't want to go home. I should really drop your ass off for saying that," he said as he grabbed my hand and pulled me out the chair.

****

When we stepped inside his apartment, I was impressed at how clean he kept it for a man. He had nice furniture too, and it was even decorated. Matter of fact, it was some nice shit in this nigga's spot.

"Do you have a job or something? I mean, I don't want to be nosey, but you have a lot of nice things. You're even pushing a Mercedes," I said, rubbing my hand across a cheetah statue on an end table.

He walked back into his room and I followed him. I saw the remote for the TV on the bed, so I grabbed it and made myself at home.

"Well, damn, you can't even ask first before you go grabbing shit?" he asked as he lay down behind me.

I noticed he ignored my question. The only reason he would ignore it was if he was moving some shit. He was a rare jewel.

"I didn't think I had to," I said.

I scooted my butt on him, and he started to move his hands up and down on my thighs. I caught his hand.

"I told you no punani," I said and moved his hand.

"We grown, girl. Damn, I promise you I been around plenty of slutty bitches, and they would have been tried to jump on me. You resisting and I see you a good one." He stood up.

I smiled because he was falling for my bullshit.

"Where you going?" I asked him.

"To the bathroom, if that's okay with you," he said sarcastically. He went in and closed the door behind him.

I only had a minute, so I went to his side drawer where I knew he had to have condoms. I was right. He had a three pack of Magnums in there. I looked around in the drawer until I found a football ribbon, and just my luck, it had a pin in it. I pricked holes in all the condoms, stuck the pin back in the ribbon, and laid back down. I heard the bathroom door open, and I was chilling by the time he came back in.

I sat up and pulled him down to me. "I don't usually do this, but you're different."

I shoved my tongue in his mouth and started rubbing his dick through his shorts. When I felt the monster he'd been hiding in there, I knew this shit was about to be bomb.

"You sure?" he said as he kissed my neck and pulled down my jumper straps.

"Yeah, I'm sure."

He went into the dresser and pulled out one of the condoms. I smirked and laid back, waiting to get pregnant and live the good life.

Milan

Walking across campus had my legs burning, and I wasn't even near the hall I needed to be at for my class. My book bag was so heavy it almost toppled me over. I saw Natasha standing by the benches talking to some guy, so I decided to let her get her chill on and kept it moving.

When I finally made it where I needed to be, I was stuck for a minute before going in after seeing something that made my stomach turn. I saw India walking with Cain, and she looked like she couldn't be happier, and was obviously making a lot of girls jealous from a few faces I saw. He saw me looking and he nodded at me, but I just went ahead inside.

Cain had switched up on me quick. He was chatty and nice at first, but now he just head nods me. That's okay, he wants to be with a hoe, well he had the hoe of all hoes now.

My class was complete ear torture as professor Banh gave his most boring lecture yet. This was a journalism class, yet we only listened to him talk about the times he wrote for the New York Times. I was tired of hearing of it and wanted to learn something from him besides how many articles he put out. Once I saw my phone's clock, I jumped up and left. He also had a thing about going past the time, and I wasn't having it. I still had to go print this paper for my next class. In a rush to make it to the library before my next class, I dashed like I was running for the gold. I got in and out quickly, which was a surprise because it was usually crowded.

On the way, I saw Marquise talking to some of the football players, including Cain. I didn't want him to see me, so I tried to move fast, but ended up clipping over somebody's book bag that they carelessly had sitting on the grass. I heard laughter erupt, and the loudest cackle came from my own sister. Marquise and Cain both started to run over, but I saw India grab Cain's arm.

"You okay?" Marquise said, trying to help me up.

"I'm fine. I don't need any help."

I was still hurt by his words at the club the other night, and I didn't want shit from him, not even a helping hand.

"I'm sorry about the other night. I was still mad as fuck that you killed my baby and didn't even have the sense to tell me. Then, I see you partying and shit. It just fucked me up."

I saw Cain still watching, but India kept trying to get his attention.

"That's all well and good, but you didn't have to do that. You don't think you put me through enough, Mar?" I hadn't called him Mar since I caught his ass cheating. That's was my nickname for him.

"Yes, but in all honesty, I think we should try to start over, bae. Look how good we had it. Tell me you don't love me, and I swear I will never bother you again," he said with his gorgeous face fixed on mine.

"I do love you, I ju—"

Before I could finish my sentence, he kissed me and I started to cry. It seemed like all the pain from me having the abortion down to him cheating, came rushing back.

"I'm sorry I hurt you, Milan. I swear, I'm gonna spend every day making this shit up to you."

I looked over at Cain and my sister wrapped her arms around him. I shook my head and put on a smile.

"You better not."

He got so excited, he screamed. "Yes! Thank you, baby. I love you."

"I love you too," I said and kissed him.

We walked past my sister and the rest of the team. I felt a little bit better knowing I at least had somebody to be there for me. I was gonna give him one more chance, and I swear he better not do me wrong again. Deep down, I knew I was making a mistake in rushing to take him back, but I hoped I was wrong.

*****

"Congratulation, Milan, you're gonna make a great journalist when you graduate," my dean said as she handed me the award I had won for my article in the paper.

I was trying not to focus on her coffee stained teeth and cigarette breath, but it was undeniably strong.

"I appreciate this, thank you so much," I said with a smile.

All of the school's paper staff clapped and cheered me on. Everyone went to their desks, and I went and sat at mine. I took a picture of the award and sent it to my mother. Of course, she sent back kisses, and that made me smile. I saw my editor coming over, so I put my phone down and gave him my attention.

"Hey, Milan. Okay, so you know we do a story every year on the graduating athletes. We took one from every sport, and we are giving you the honor of writing the story. Oh, and did I mention it will be featured in ESPN magazine?" he said.

"Oh my God, are you serious? Why me?" I asked, getting excited to be featured in a major magazine.

"You really have to ask? So, graduation is coming, and I need you to start with Abdul Wilshire, then Jonothan Dunlap," he said, tapping his hand with his pen. "And save Cain Wilson for last. We need to see who he is going with when he leaves. His coach gave me an off the record that he could be getting drafted."

When he said Cain's name, my stomach tightened for some reason.

"Okay, thanks for the opportunity." I put on a smile as he walked away.

I bit on my pen and got ready to go to class. I knew I had to do a good job with this story. This was my chance to be seen for the first time, and after that, who knows what could happen? I left out the building and started walking to my last class, and I was all smiles. I saw Marquise walking with a few of his friends, so I walked up and gave him a kiss.

"Wassup, sexy." He smiled and wrapped his arms around my waist. "I'ma get with y'all niggas later," he told his friends.

"So, I thought about what you asked me yesterday, and I want to go," I said, referring to the trip he and his friends were taking next month.

"Dope! I'ma make sure we get the cabin with the big bed. We gonna need it," he said and kissed me on the cheek.

I saw Cain walking across campus and I tried not to stare, but I noticed he was looking right back at my ass. I bit down on my lip and tried to pay attention to Marquise, but my eyes kept drifting to Cain until he was out of sight.

****

The next day I was sitting on the couch watching TV in my mother's living room and I heard India throwing up in the bathroom again for the second time since I'd been there. I was waiting for my mother to get back with the rental car she had got for me until my car gets fixed.

I knocked on the door, and she swung it open with a scowl on her face.

"You okay?" I asked and grabbed a paper towel for her.

"Yeah, thanks." She took the paper towel from me and wiped her mouth.

I was surprised she wasn't acting like her usual nasty self.

"You sick?" I asked.

"No, nosey, I'm pregnant, I think," she said and walked into her room and lay on the bed.

"By who?" I asked. For some reason, I hoped like hell it wasn't Cain's.

"Cain is the obvious answer. Damn, you can go now," she said and waved me off.

I turned around and immediately felt the knot in my stomach. The front door opened and my mother walked in with a huge smile on her face.

"Hey honey, you okay?" she asked.

"Yeah, yeah. I just remembered I have to go do this paper," I lied. I just wanted to get the hell out of there. How the hell did she get a guy like him?

I kissed my mother's cheek and she handed me the key with the plastic tag on it. I went out saw that she had rented what looked like a brand new jeep. I jumped in, adjusted my mirrors, and left. I hated I was feeling jealous, even though I had somebody already. I turned on my Pandora and listened to Adele on the ride home.

When I pulled into the parking lot, I saw Cain and some light skinned girl walking into the gates of the complex. I had seen her on campus before. I drove by and didn't bother to try to speak or anything. I felt mad at him for some reason. I got out of the jeep, and when I got closer to them, I could see him watching me, but I just kept going.

I could feel his eyes on me, but I kept marching up the steps. Finally reaching my apartment, I went in and slammed the door. It was quiet, so I assumed that Natasha wasn't home. I threw my purse in my desk chair and turned my TV on. The thought of calling Marquise crossed my mind, but what was I gonna say? *Hey babe, I'm jealous that my sister is pregnant by that fine ass Cain.* No. So, I decided not to even bother calling. I just lay down and let the TV play while I day dreamed about how much I couldn't stand him now. The lies we tell ourselves.

Cain

"Yo, I need you to come to the crib when you get a chance," I told my man, Ju.

I needed him to run something over to my lil niggas. I needed the to flip this shit quick because I felt like we had the shit too long, and they needed to tighten up, or I was gonna tighten they ass up. I had let India in on my shit because she was so eager to please. I had her ass vialing up and everything.

I turned back toward the table to see if she had that pack ready, and her ass was gone. This was a lazy ass broad. She thought since I hit the joint that I was supposed to wife her and shit. I wasn't wifing nobody I didn't want to, and I certainly wasn't wifing her ass.

I walked in the bedroom of the trap house and went to the bathroom. I knocked and India opened the door with a smile.

"Can you believe we're going to have a baby?" India said, jumping around holding the pregnancy test in her hand.

I didn't want to seem like a motherfucker, but I wasn't happy about this shit at all. I didn't want to have a baby right now, and on some real shit, I ain't want a baby with her ass. She was a fuckin' liar and was only good for bagging my shit up. I had found out all that shit she told me about Milan was a fucking lie after I decided to holla at Marquise one day after a game.

We had all sat in the locker room talking, and Marquise started talking about his girl, Milan. I didn't even know he was with her until that day she fell and he ran up. Anyway, he said he got her a ring and all kinds of shit, and I was so surprised he would deal with a chick who was hoeing. I pretty much flat out asked the nigga why he would fuck with a chick like that. It seemed like everybody knew her but me, and they all said she was a nerd and a good girl. It confused me because of what India told me about her and the fact that I found those pills just made more believable. So, that bitch straight lied for no reason. I don't respect liars, and this bitch was no exception.

I ended up talking to Marquise when we were alone and told him my bad. When I told him what was said to me, he shook his head. He even said she was a virgin when they first started talking. That was a blow to me. I wish I would have given her a chance on my own, and now this nigga had her back, and it was too late. I knew I had a good feeling about her, and it helped that she wasn't the overexposed type of chick. She dressed in jeans and t-shirts, but she still looked like a goddess.

"Aren't you gonna say anything, Cain?" India asked.

"Are you ready for a baby? I mean, damn, you just graduated and I'm about to leave the damn state. On some real shit, I don't want no damn baby," I told her.

"I know. The baby can come with us."

I was confused by this *us* thing. This broad was on bullshit, and I didn't get how she thought I even treated her like I wanted to be with her.

"What you mean 'us'? We only been around each other for a month or some shit. And it ain't been no cuffing shit, either." I shook my head and grabbed my phone out my pocket to check the message I just got.

"So, I was just a fuck to you then, huh? You're just like the rest. I open myself to you, and you shit on me." She started crying and it made me feel like an asshole.

"I'm just saying, you are a fuck, remember? I don't plan to get married and shit no time soon. I ain't ready for all that, and it wouldn't be with you anyway. But if you want to have the baby, I will help you out and shit, but ain't no us, shawty."

"So, you're gonna run off and just leave us here so you can live the good life? Wow, Cain. I thought you were better than that." She grabbed her purse and shoes, and went stomping out.

"India!" I walked out the room and following her to the door.

"What, Cain?" she said with her back turned.

I could hear her sniffling, so I turned her around and she buried her head in my stomach.

"First the fuck off, I know you don't call yourself walking the fuck away from me when I'm talking."

"So, I'm just gonna be a single mother struggling and shit?"

I didn't even say shit back. Like I said, if I had created a child, I was gonna take care of it. I still didn't know how it happened because I knew I strapped up every time.

She tried to hug me, but I pushed her off. I was kind of wondering a few things for real. I hadn't fucked her in like three weeks, so how far along was she? She had a nigga like me fucked up.

Shaking my head, I thought about how I wouldn't be able to play for my dream team. I was starting to feel more and more that this bitch had motives. The truth always comes out, and she better enjoy this shit while she can. Always said I wouldn't let myself fuck up like this if I ever had a chance to go pro, but here I was. Damn.

*****

I had just left my last class and I was ready to finally graduate from this bitch. Straight hitta got a fucking degree! I'm a new breed of hood nigga. Graduation was coming, and I just knew I would get in the draft. If I didn't, I would go to medical school and be a surgeon or some shit. Probably not, though. I only started school to play ball. I wasn't interested in being in no damn medical shit. I was good either way, but since I loved ball, I knew that would put me where I wanted to be.

After dapping up a few of my classmates, I rolled out. I stopped in the dorms and handed off the bookbag I was carrying to my school runner, Craps. He had been my homie since freshman year, and I planned to pass him the connect when I pulled out this shit.

"Hey, Cain."

A cute a light skinned joint waved as she came out the building. I waved her over and got her number so I could make sure to holla at her ass later. I watched her cute ass bounce off, and I went in to handle my business. I know y'all thinking I'm a hoe or a nigga thot, but nah. I just wasn't gay, and I was gonna get pussy for sure, though. I wasn't running through them like everybody thought I was, but when I saw a piece like shawty that just passed me, I couldn't let her go without some Cain in her life.

I knocked on the door, and this nigga Craps answered, sweating like a crack head and shit. Butt ass naked.

"Nigga, what the fuck? You think I wanna see that shit?" I said as I handed him the bag and gritted on him.

I didn't even want to wonder what the fuck this nigga had going on.

Cain

I was standing in the student union talking shit to UCLA's basketball point guard when I saw Milan walking down the stairs. She had braids like Janet Jackson had in Poetic Justice.

"Aye, I'ma holla at you later, aight?" I told Brenden, and then ran to catch up with Milan.

"Milan." I touched her shoulder and she jumped. I realized I had scared her. She had headphones in, so she probably didn't hear me come up.

"Hi Cain. This is crazy, I was just about to go talk to the coach about you!" she screamed.

I pulled her headphones out. She realized she must have been loud, and covered her mouth as she laughed.

"It's cool, you almost blew my eardrum, though. Now why were you seeing the coach about me?" I asked.

"Because, I'm doing the story on the senior athletes, so you're kind of up next," she said with a slight smile.

"Oh, well that's wassup. We can start whenever."

"Okay, good."

We got quiet, and it felt awkward as shit.

"Hey, did you get a notice on your door about smoking weed in the buildings?" I pretty much said anything to start a conversation.

"Yeah, I saw. It was probably my roommate and you." She laughed and flipped her hair back.

"Let you tell it. So, you a senior now, or…" I felt like a fucking idiot.

I really didn't know why I stopped her, and I didn't even know what the hell I was trying to say, but I didn't give a fuck as long as her cute ass rapped to me.

"I'm a junior. One more year left, and I'm outta here. I'm jealous of you guys."

"No need, I'm sure you gon' knock it out. I heard you were smart," I said, feeling more comfortable talking to her.

"What, you been asking around? I thought I did something wrong since you started switching up on me." She bit her bottom lip, which was the cutest shit I'd ever seen. Damn, I hoped my dick didn't get hard.

"Well, let me just apologize about that. I was misinformed about some things and... I'm just sorry, aight. Don't hold it against a nigga."

"It's cool, you don't owe me anything, Cain," she said, sounding like Christmas music saying my name.

"So, where you headed?" I asked as I ran my hand through her braid.

"I was going to get some food then go to work."

"Oh, well I'm hungry as hell too. Where we going?" I asked, boldly inviting myself. I wasn't cracking on her; I was just being nice because of how much of a jackass I was. Lies, I was making a move on her ass.

"I was going to Panda Express."

"Ugh, you eat that nasty shit? We can go to Plateau; I love the oysters there."

"Okay, that's cool," she said and readjusted her bag.

We walked to the pavilion and got a table in the corner. After we got our food, we got deep into conversation. Then, she shocked me and had me stuck on stupid.

"So, congrats on the baby," she said, while picking up some of her salad.

I was stuck, I didn't think she knew.

"Oh." I shrugged.

"Don't look so happy."

"I'm not happy at all. I got plans. I don't love her or even have any intention of fuckin' with her on that level, and I don't want to get her hopes up like we were gonna be in something serious. She your sister, let her know it's dead."

"Try to go through Satan because that's the only person that demon listens to." She laughed. "Okay, I really don't know. We don't get along too well, so I don't know what to tell you, Cain."

"I can see y'all don't."

I didn't want to run my mouth like a bitch, so I decided to keep quiet about what India told me. We ended up having a good conversation, and I had to admit that this girl was amazing. Her goals in life had me in chills because I had never seen anybody so level headed and determined. Fuck, I wish I would have got to her first.

"Well, thanks for lunch, Cain. I'm glad we did this. I guess since we're gonna be somewhat family now, it's cool." She flashed that pretty smile and backed away.

I didn't want her ass to leave. "Well, I'll be home at like 8:30. You wanna chill or something? Empire comes on tonight."

I couldn't believe I just said some dumb shit like that. I don't even watch that shit, I just know females do. I had seen the damn commercial in Coach's office. I must have sounded like a pussy.

"I don't know. Marquise wouldn't like that," she said, turning me down.

It wasn't like me and him were best friends and shit, we just happened to play on the same team. But I felt what she was saying. Plus, I had fucked around and got her sister pregnant, but fuck that, baby was mine. I was about to full court press her ass too.

"Girl, you act like I'm trying to smash or something. I just thought we was cool now, so it was aight to chill. You live damn near next door." I walked closer. I couldn't wait to give her some dick. She looked like she needed some good nuts.

"Okay, fine. I have to study, though, so as soon as it goes off, I gotta run."

"You can study with me," I quickly put in. For some reason my mind went straight to her getting back shots.

"Damn, boy, you got somebody robbing my apartment or something? You trying to keep me out the house, I see." She laughed.

Maybe I was pushing it. "You right. We can watch the show, and then you can go study so you can be like me one day. I'm in building 12, apartment 201." I said and walked off.

I had a little smile on my face, she had really made an impression on me. I needed shawty something serious.

*****

"Yes, daddy," Mimi moaned while I was diving into that pussy.

I pulled my dick out and stuck it into her mouth. She was swallowing as much as she could, and doing it with no effort. She was the light skinned joint I had met at the dorms. A stone cold freak, and I was taking full advantage of that right now. She sucked my dick like she was hungry for dick, and her throat was velvet. I started banging on her mouth until I felt my nut build up, then I released my cum down her throat. Once I pulled my dick out her mouth, I grabbed a towel the maids had left on the bed.

I didn't take her ass to my place because I didn't want another India type hoe on my hands, who thought since I had her in the crib that she could show up whenever. India had come to my damn house unannounced a few days ago, and I went south on her ass. So, now, the only chick I was bringing up in there was Milan. I was after her ass something serious. I was actually about to pick her up from work because her car was acting up and shit. I had no problems doing that shit. I had to get her at noon.

"So, what you doing the rest of the day?" Mimi came in the bathroom when I started the shower.

"Bout ta go pick this shawty up and make some moves," I said honestly. I ain't have no reason to lie.

"Damn, you just gonna say that shit to me like that?" she asked with her arms folded.

She was still naked, and her titties were sitting pretty as shit. Almost made me wanna fuck again, but I didn't want to be late getting Milan.

It's been about a week since she came to my place to kick it with a nigga, and we've been cooling like shit. I could tell I was getting in her head, if I wasn't already there. I was cuffing Milan and soon. She had said something to the effect of hanging with me felt like cheating, so was kinda waiting on Marquise to fuck up so she wouldn't feel like she was cheating and shit.

Mimi slammed the door, breaking me out of my thoughts and shit. I laughed and got in the shower. Her ass should be gone by the time I got out. I got clean and made sure my balls were fresh and everything else. After I brushed my teeth and combed my beard, I left out the bathroom. Mimi was gone, thank God. She seemed like she was about to get in her feelings and shit, and I didn't want to hear it. I grabbed my clothes out the duffle I brought and got dressed.

After I texted Milan to tell her I was on the way, I left the room and got the valet to bring my car around. When the nigga pulled up, I hopped in and tipped him $5, then I made my way to Milan's fine ass. I pulled into a space and walked down until I got to the Starbucks. I saw her cute ass behind the counter and decided to fuck with her.

"Can I get some of you with whip cream?" I asked.

She looked up and smiled.

"You silly. I'm ready to go, let me punch out."

Her lil coworkers looked jealous as hell.

"Ain't you Cain?" the one who was staring the hardest asked.

"Yeah, why?"

"I just didn't know you was messing with Milan." She scrunched her face up and the other girls started snickering.

"I'd rather fuck with her than y'all bucket head ass bitches." I smirked and Milan came walking back down toward me on the customer side.

"Ready?" she asked.

I took her bookbag from her and the other one she was carrying.

"Aww, thanks," she said as we walked to the door.

I went out first and held it for her. She was all smiles as she walked out.

"No problem."

"So, what's wrong with your whip?" I asked as I loaded her stuff into my car.

"Everything," she said in an exasperated tone.

"I can get you something nice if you need it, shawty. Money ain't really an issue," I said as I cranked my car up.

Push it, push it, push it. Go get the money, go get the money.

My O.T. Genesis ringtone went off and I saw it was somebody I didn't get many phone calls from. My connect, also known as my father.

"Yeah?" I answered.

"You need to come home," he said.

Something must have happened. Home wasn't what you'd think it was. Home was the park down the street from his house. He felt that if the police were ever tapping his phone, they would be confused.

"Aight." I hung up

"You need to go home right now? If you do, that's cool, but if you run with me, I can take you to eat or something," I asked Milan.

"Well I sure could eat so its whatever you say Cain." She said sounding all sweet and shit.

"I like that." I said nodding and looking forward.

I made it to Cesar Chavez playground and made sure the air was on before I got out the car.

"Be right back, sweetheart."

"Okay." She giggled as she blushed, due me calling her sweetheart, I'm sure.

I closed the door and walked over to my pops.

"Who you got in your car?" he asked without even speaking and shit first.

"My business. So, what's up."

"I got a call from your man, Craps. Motherfucka called me like he had some kind of juice or some shit. Talkin' bout y'all need more weight. Thought you was runnin' shit," he said in a way that let me know he wanted me to fuck Craps up. I didn't disagree because the nigga was way out of line.

"I got you."

"So, you gonna stick to this football shit? I wanna know because I ain't bout ta keep going, so I need somebody to run this shit.

"I fucks with the hustle and you know that, Pops, but I ain't trying to be at this shit my whole life."

"But it's for you, Cain. You got power, boy, and you need to flex it, nigga. This what we do. You really see yourself bein' a fuckin' doctor? I mean, shit, football dope, but how long you gonna play? You need to build something, lil' nigga." He got up and slid me a key.

"Grab that, and bump somebody else up to your right hand." He walked away.

I wasn't bout ta do Milan dirty and ride with all the shit I was about to pick up.

"I'm taking you somewhere nice. Go home and change, and I will pick you up in about two hours.

"Okay, cool, dag. I ain't know it was this nice having a man for a friend," she said.

"Just wait 'til I'm your man," I said boldly.

"I got a man, remember?" she seemed unconvinced her damn self.

Marquise ain't shit, but since I ain't a bitch nigga, all I could do was slide up between they ass. He stays with different bitches, that's why I ain't know they was even doing shit at first. He said some hoe was pregnant, and she showed up in the locker room with the baby and shit. He tried to play like she was on some groupie shit, but he ain't fool nobody with that bullshit.

"I hear you talkin', but you bout ta go get cute as fuck for me, ain't you?" I said and looked over at her. She was red as hell.

"Well, what if I don't go?" She snapped her neck.

"Don't be ready when I pull up, and watch."

"Well, you gonna be disappointed."

She kept faking. Little did she know, I would snatch her lil' ass up if she was ready when I got there. When I pulled up in front of her building, I went around and opened the door for her.

"You got all the way out the car just to let me out?" she asked, kind of making me feel bad for her. Clearly, she never got treated like a woman should.

"Yeah, you need a nigga like me, shawty. Go get pretty and shit, and be ready when I come back."

I hugged her and she went inside with a big ass smile on her face. Her as was about to be spoiled rotten. I was taking her to Venice Beach just to cool it for a minute, then to Oliver's Prime. I needed me a big as steak right about now. I hurried to the storage place and went to the unit that he must have just gotten somebody to purchase. We change them out every so often so nobody would catch a routine.

I backed my car in and popped my trunk open so I could load everything into the trunk. I had to ask that buckethead bitch India to help my cousin, Kimbella, and break this shit down. My nigga, Zay, stays in the trap most of the time, so he would make sure they were on point. Plus, I had a few cameras that you couldn't even see in the spot. I just needed to make sure my money was on point because I wasn't in the business of losing a motherfuckin' thing.

"Yo, I need you to meet Kimbella at the spot, man. I got some bread for you," I said to India on the phone.

"Mmm, and what you about to do?"

I hung up and called Milan. I wasn't about to engage in any type of conversation because she wouldn't stop.

"Yo, I'm about to go home and get my shit together. I'ma be there, aight?" I said and waited for her to respond.

"I don't think I can go. I really don't—"

I hung up and headed over to her ass. I told her I wasn't playing. I pulled up in front of her building and went straight to her and Natasha's door. I could smell the fragrance of that Febreeze air freshener they use. I knew it because my stepmother used the same one at my father's house.

"Who is it?" I heard Natasha yell. She must have pressed her face against the peephole because I heard the thud.

"Oh," I heard her squeal. She swung the door open and stood there smiling from ear to ear.

"Hey, Cain."

I looked past her and smiled when I saw Milan emerge.

She had changed and apparently got dressed up just like I asked her to.

"I was just playing. You didn't have to come by now," she said, grabbing her bag and walking out with me.

"Bitch, answer your text," Natasha yelled out behind us.

"So, you was gonna make me go?" she asked while we walked down the stairs.

"Pretty much. Now you gotta stop at my place so I can get changed.

"You look good the way you are," she said, looking me over. I guess I was good.

"Why you being so nice to me all of a sudden?" she asked out the blue.

"I just fuck with you. You cool as fuck," I let her know.

"Oh, well I feel bad because I hope it don't look like I'm cheating. Even though he did." She rolled her eyes.

"Well, why you get back with him? I mean, it ain't my business, but you too good for somebody to bullshit you around." I spoke to her truthfully.

"I know, I just hate being lonely. My whole life, nobody paid me any attention except my mother. Then Marquise came in my life and showed me all the attention, and I just fell for a dream." She shrugged.

"It's all good, but for real, though. If I had a shawty like you, it would be easy living for whoever she is," I said, continuing the drive.

Tonight was gonna be my first move.

India

I had tried my best to keep Cain interested in me, but it seemed like all he wanted me to do as work for him. That wasn't the role I signed up for. At least it was getting me some money, and that was good, since I was dealing with a bunch of broke niggas. I needed to step my game up. I couldn't believe he really tried to leave without taking me with him. I was so happy when I got that test and it came back positive. I was about to be a baller's wife, shit, even a hustler's wife. I was glad I had the upper hand in life, and I wouldn't have to even go to school now.

I heard my phone going off, and when I picked it up to see my mother calling, I just slid the end button. Brian was snoring in my face and his breath smelled like dog shit. I got up and put on his t-shirt, then grabbed a towel out his closet. I needed to hurry up and leave so I could make it to my doctor's appointment.

When I got into the bathroom I started the shower and waited for it to heat up before I jumped in. I was using his mother's Dove body wash, and I always loved the way that smelled. There was a knock on the door. I figured it was Brian, so I got out, soapy and all, and unlocked the door then started to walk back.

"Sheeeeesh. Damn, lil mama. That lil nigga can't be fuckin' that pussy right." I turned around to see Chance standing there holding his dick.

"I thought you were Brian. You betta get outta here before your old lady come and catch you." I smirked and got back in, making sure I gave him a good view of my ass before closing the glass shower door.

"She gone to work."

He licked his lips and walked up to the shower, watching me soap up the rag and rub it all over my titties. I pushed it between my legs and started to wash my pussy. I gave him the whole freak show. I guess he couldn't take my teasing anymore because he stripped down and got in with me. His body was heavenly, and when I saw that dick swing, baaaaabbbyyyy. I knew I was a hoe for sure because he was about to get this pregnant pussy. I had good dickdar; I was always right about every dude I ever had sex with. They had nice, long, porn star dicks, and that's all I wanted on my dick team.

"Eat it," I said and propped my legs up on the soap holder. He got right down and pushed his head between my legs. I was shaking already. He had a nice long tongue so he was pushed it in and out of my hole like it was a dick. I kept grinding on his face until I felt my orgasm built up, and I came on his face. I grinded up and down so I could cum all over it.

"Shit," I said as I put my legs down, still shaking from the orgasm.

"Bend that shit over." He grabbed me by the face and shoved his tongue in my mouth, then he turned me around and started violently smacking my ass.

"You a nasty a bitch, ain't you?" he asked as he roughly pushed inside me. I clenched my eyes closed as he fucked me like an animal. My body was doing flips and I could feel my juices pushing out as I came all over his dick.

"Mmmmhmm, cum on this dick, bitch." He turned me to face him again, and he picked me up and slammed me against the wall.

I wrapped both legs around his large frame and held on as he dug into me. I didn't even give a fuck that Brian was in the other room, I screamed out in ecstasy as Chance beat my pussy into a coma. I was in love with the dick already.

"Fuuuuck, I'm boutta cum again." I moaned.

"Yeah, I know, that's what I do."

His cocky ass was slamming his dick into me and pressing hard, then holding it in for a minute. My eyes rolled in the back of my head, and I swear I saw the light. I was dead for sure because I was in heaven. I'd had some good dick in my short time fucking, and this nigga is definitely top two material. I felt his dick start to pulse, and I knew he was about to cum. I pulled up and let him nut between my ass cheeks.

"You need to come around more often," he said, getting out and scooping his clothes up. He walked out ass naked, and I wanted to follow for some more.

I continued my shower with a big satisfied grin across my face, and then went back in the room with Brian and got dressed. He was still sleep, so I kissed him, then left. Chance was sitting in the living room rolling a when I walked past the living room.

"Aye," he called out for me.

"Yeah?" I asked with a smirk.

"Come here," he said and closed the blunt.

I walked over to him and he pulled me down and kissed me as he rubbed between my legs. I started to gey wet all over again. I knew I had to get out of there because could I could take that dick all day.

"I gotta go." I hurried out the door to my car. I was hot, and I needed to cool the hell off.

I drove to my doctor's appointment happy to check on the baby. I called Cain and he didn't answer, so I sent him a text and told him not to be late. When I checked in with the nurse they had me fill out forms and everything since it was my first appointment. I saw all the women in there with the big bellies and I couldn't wait until my stomach got like theirs.

I checked my phone to see if Cain had hit me back, and he hadn't. Where the hell was he?

The nurse came out after about fifteen minutes and called me to the back. I looked at the door to see if Cain was coming in, and nope. Nothing. I felt so stupid, I should have had the nigga fall in love, then trap him with the baby. At least I knew my child support checks would be fat if he didn't want to be with me.

They took blood, and then I had to pee in a cup. She led me to a room at the end of the hall after everything else was taken care of.

"I need you to strip down and put this on," she said and placed a gown on the bed.

"Okay." She left out and I started to change.

The knock on the door made me jump, and I went and peeked out. It was Cain. He had to duck to get in the door. His big ass was sexy as fuck.

"Your sister's car broke down, and I offered her a ride to the enterprise." He said like it was no big deal.

I started feel furious and knew I was about to pop off. "You telling me you were late coming to our child's first appointment because my stupid ass sister's piece of shit broke down!" I screamed.

"Bitch, you need to calm the fuck down and stop screaming at me like I'm a fuckin' child. I don't know who the fuck you thought I was, but you betta believe I'm Cain!" he barked at me.

It sounded like he was growling. I had never seen him angry.

"I'm just saying. You act like you don't care? I told you she was a hoe. I bet she tried to have sex you, didn't she?" I said, trying to sound pitiful.

"I ain't finna go back and forth with you about your sister. She's doing a story on me, and she's cool as fuck, so that's all you need to know. I already know you was lying about the other shit, so stop it. That's why I don't trust your trifling ass. Yeah, I said that, so don't look fuckin' surprised."

What the hell did he mean by that? She must have got to him. That bitch.

"Fine, Cain. If the baby isn't more important than my sister th—"

He opened the door and left out. Damn, I thought that would pull some sympathy for sure. I called his phone and he must have ended the call because it rang twice and went to voicemail.

"Cain, can you please just answer the phone? I'm sorry," I said and hung up.

A few minutes later, Cain came back into the room.

"I left my honey bun in the car," he said, then sat down and tore off the top. "You want a piece?" He offered.

I shook my head, then his phone beeped. He opened it and looked confused.

"I didn't even hear my phone ring," he said and put it back in his pocket.

"I thought you left," I said, feeling stupid for calling and whining into the phone. I didn't want him to get angry again, so I didn't say shit about all the other stuff he said.

"You need to chill out. You the one stressing the baby," he said as he wolfed down the honey bun. The doctor came in, and I was like *damn*. He was a sexy ass white dude. I stopped noticing his look and noticed he had a concerned look on his face.

"I need to speak with her privately, sir. Are you her husband?" he asked Cain.

"Hell no," he said flat out. He didn't even say I was his girl or nothing.

"Oh, well, do you mind?" he was asking Cain to step out.

Cain got up and walked out the room.

"Is something wrong with the baby?" I asked, wondering why he needed Cain to leave.

"No, but when the nurse was about to check your urine she noticed some blood."

"Oh my God. What does that mean?"

"We want to swab you and check you for some things, and since it's so early, we want to check you into labor and delivery, just until we straighten things out. So, I'm about to swab you and then check your cervix."

I would die if I lost my meal ticket.

"Do whatever you have to."

The nurse came back in and told me that my boyfriend was waiting in the lobby. She brought in a sonogram machine and I laid back waiting for the doctor once again. When he finally came back he sat down and squirted jelly all over my stomach. He clicked and moved around with the tool.

"Okay, so your paperwork says your last period was last month, but you seem to be almost 16 weeks."

"Wait, that's not right. I was still having cycles. My stomach isn't even big," I said with my heart beating out my chest. This baby couldn't be Cain's. I wasn't with him yet.

"I'm sure. From the measurements and the size of the fetus, it's accurate. Some people don't show until later."

I wanted to cry. I wasn't showing or anything to be four months pregnant.

"Okay."

That was all I could say. I hadn't fucked anybody worth a damn since Cain, and I wasn't about to be a baby mother to some bum.

"You can get dressed. We need to get you to the hospital."

"Thanks," I said as he left the the room.

What the fuck was I gonna do?

Milan

"Sis, you ready?" Natasha called from her room to me.

I had my hair up in a messy bun, and I opted to wear a cute pair of cutoff jeans and a halter top. Since living with Natasha, she had changed my way of dressing. I always wore jeans and a t shirt, but I had started to see myself as more beautiful, so I kicked it up. I still won't do over the top makeup, but I wore a little.

I checked myself in the mirror and made sure I felt good about what was looking back and I was set. We were going to the football team's party to celebrate the seniors who were graduating. Since we were going on the trip tomorrow, I made sure I packed a bag to bring. I was going to stay with Marquise tonight so we could leave with everybody. I heard familiar voices in the living room, and like déjà vu, I walked in and saw Mariah and Janay sitting on the couch watching TV and smoking.

"Hey y'all," I said walking out, and sitting next to them on the couch.

"Damn, look at ole girl. You must have thought Cain was gonna be here," Janay said and laughed.

"What? Why would you think that? My sister messing with him anyway," I said as I crossed my legs.

"Mmmm, no offense, but your sister ain't making the best impression on our family. I love my cousin and he's free to make his own choices, but I don't trust her," Mariah said honestly.

"I wouldn't trust her either," I grumbled under my breath.

"But Cain seems to like you, though," Mariah retorted.

"He's a cool dude," I said, being nonchalant but still blushing.

"Well, I heard y'all watched Empire." They both busted out laughing.

"How the hell you get Cain to watch some shit like that? you must have put some pussy on him or something," Janay chimed in.

"Um no, we was studying and stuff. You know, chillin'."

They looked at each other and high fived.

"Sis, he bout ta get you together real quick," Mariah said and tapped my leg. I didn't even know what the hell that meant.

"So, he really a drug dealer?" I blurted out.

They looked at me like I had said something wrong.

"You can't be saying shit like that. My cousin do what he gotta do, but he a good dude. Don't let him hear you say no shit like that," Janay said in a serious tone.

I didn't even respond.

"Okay, y'all, fuck all that. Let's go be the baddest bitches in the building," Natasha yelled as she grabbed her keys and headed to the door.

We all left out and got into her new Nissan that her mother had bought her. We played some music and talked about who all would be there until we got to the Ritz Carlton. Valet took the car down and we headed inside. The lobby was full of people I recognized from school. They were all headed in the same direction, so we just followed them. I hated that I didn't come with Marquise, but a bunch of the players had rented a party bus and took it over.

When we got inside the ballroom, we heard the usual frat calls and guys stepping around. A lot of the football players were laughing and pressing up on females. It was a nice setup too, they had a full buffet and a DJ.

"I'm ready to get down with some of these drinks," Natasha and started to dance to the music.

I saw Marquise standing over at the bar talking to some girl. I didn't want to jump to conclusions, so I started walking over, but the girl had already walked off.

"Hey, baby, you made it," he said nervously.

"So, who was that?" I asked, pointing in the direction the girl had gone.

"Just some girl who at the party, babe. It's nothing," he said and kissed me. "I gave you this promise ring because I meant what I said."

I smiled and looked at what he called a promise ring. It was a nice sized diamond that looked more like an engagement ring.

"Yeah, same thing you always say."

"Yeah, yeah." He kissed me again.

"I hate to interrupt the love birds, but we about to get to this buffet. Save you a seat, okay?" Natasha said.

I waved, and when I was turning back to Marquise, I saw Cain come in. He was a cool guy for the most part. I laughed my ass off at the fact that he was watching Empire with me that night. I could tell he really wasn't into it, but I guess he was just trying to relate to me or something. I had completed his story and we were still cool.

"What's good, bruh?" Marquise said in his thick Philly accent.

"Nothing much, just chillin' for now. How you doing, Ms. Journalist?" Cain said, turning his attention from Marquise to me. I felt that look.

"Same thing as you, I guess." I smiled.

We, of course, had to be on the low about how we'd been going out and stuff. I almost felt like I was ready to let Marquise go because I didn't think it was fair.

"Look at you," I heard India say as she walked up. She was looking me up and down then she started laughing. "You got the tag on your shirt." She snatched it off and cracked up.

I'd had enough of her. Natasha and Mariah walked up, but I was ready to handle her on my own for once.

"Mad because I didn't have to fuck somebody to buy it, like you do?" I shot back.

Her face went blank and her mouth was wide open. Cain raised his eyebrows and Marquise covered his mouth, I could hear everybody snickering.

Natasha was about to say something when I saw India's father, Marshall, come toward us.

"Hey, Milan, look at you, beautiful," he said and hugged me.

"Hey, Pops,—"

"He's not your father, Milan. Your father in a crack house suckin' dick somewhere," India spat.

Marshall turned to look at her like she had lost her mind. "Are you fuckin' crazy? I am her father just as much as I am yours. I better not ever hear you disrespect your sister like that again." He chastised her like a child in front of everybody.

I had a little smirk on my face, and that pissed her off even more. She tried to pull Cain as she walked off, but he snatched his arm away from her and she was stuck on stupid. He instead walked off and sat at the bar.

Marshall shook his head and turned back to me. "I gotta go talk to some more alumnae. Let me know if you need anything, okay?" he said before kissing my cheek and walking off.

I turned back to Marquise, who was now throwing back another cup of something.

"Your sister need her ass whopped," he said after catching his breath from guzzling down his drink.

"Don't I know it. But I'm not about to let her get to me. Let's go eat," I said and pulled him over to my friends.

I saw Cain looking at me from the bar, and for some reason, I couldn't help but put on a little smile. He smiled back, but his attention was taken when India walked up. She was pouting and had her arms folded like a child. I could tell whatever she was saying was getting on his nerves.

"You hear me, girl?" Janay said, pushing my arm.

"Huh? Oh, yeah. I think so," I said diverting my eyes back to them.

"You think so what? We getting a room and we said we would be back." They started laughing.

"I'm sorry. I need to stay off this drink," I said, making an excuse for not paying attention.

"I'll be right back, bae," Marquise said, then kissed me and ran off.

I sat at the table and waited for some damn body to come back and join me. Tapping the table and bopping my head to the music while I waited, I cut my eyes back to where Cain was sitting, and he was gone. I rolled my eyes and started to just get up and grab one more drink when Cain came and sat down next to me.

"Lookin' for me?" he said with that cute smile he always wore.

"No, for what? Everybody left me, so I'm just looking around," I lied.

"Oh, I peeped that. Your stepfather a cool ass dude, but your sister wild as shit."

"Well, you brought her here." I shrugged and smirked at him.

"Nah, I didn't. She came with her father. I told you I wasn't rocking with her on that level. So, you having a good time? You look like a bomb ass meal in that outfit, shawty." He brushed the braid that fell out of my bun from my face.

I blushed and felt our electricity straight down to my toes. "Thanks, Cain, and it's cool. We haven't been here long enough to say if I'm having fun yet." I giggled then smiled.

"That smile crazy," he whispered.

I felt a brush of heat across my body, and I knew he had some type of effect on me.

"Thank you. I should find Marquise," I said, trying to escape our chemistry.

"I don't care 'bout no fuckin' Marquise. You was just chillin' with the kid last night, but see you later. Maybe you can stop by when we come back from the mountains. We can go out again." He smiled and got up with me.

"Dang, come and see me for once," I said and walked off with a smile.

Something about this felt wrong as shit. But then again, why the hell couldn't I have friends? He couldn't possibly be interested in me anyway. He was having a baby with my sister, and he was fine as hell. I was already sure he preferred a hood girl who could hold him down, and I wouldn't know shit about it. I watched him go talk to some of the guys. Damn, he looked good.

I started to look for Marquise, but he was nowhere to be found. I saw my friends up at the desk and I walked up to them to see what was going on, and to ask if they had seen this boy.

"There you go, we was just bout ta come get you," Natasha said with her arms up. Her ass was clearly drunk.

"What y'all getting a room for?" I asked.

"Because we bout ta go smoke and shit. We might be too fucked up to drive home to get our shit for the trip. I should have been smart and brought my shit like you did. But you should be worried about what you gonna be doing tonight. I saw your sorry ass man get a room," she said, shaking her head.

She still didn't like Marquise, and she had made it clear when I told her I was back with him. She said I was being stupid, and I should have let him go for good.

"He didn't say anything to me about a room. Guess it was a surprise," I said, looking around the lobby for him.

"Girl, forget that fool. We got the key, so when we done with the party, we can go the room and turn up for real!" Natatsha said.

I tried to calling him, but he didn't answer.

"There go my cousin. Cain! Come here," Mariah yelled when Cain emerged from the ballroom.

"Wassup," he said, walking over and pushing Janay.

She swatted him and pushed him back.

"You seen Marquise?" I asked Cain.

"No, not since y'all was at the table." He looked like he was lying.

"Um, okay, well if you see him, tell him I'm with them," I said, sounding pathetic, I'm sure.

"Okay," Cain said and walked off.

Janay grabbed my hand, and we all walked back in. I didn't have time to worry about him because he was obviously not worried about me.

Work, work, work, work, work work... he see me hefe work, work...

Rhianna was booming through the speakers and we all got in our girl circle and started dancing. We caught everybody's eye, and they all surrounded us and egged us on. One by one, Natasha, Mariah, and Janay got chose by some dudes, and I was left dancing alone. I wanted to leave. I was having fun, but somehow, I just kept ending up by myself.

"You wanna dance?" I heard Cain whisper in my ear from behind.

I felt like I had just been saved. He didn't even wait for me to respond before he grabbed me around the waist. We just started moving to the music. I wasn't an awesome dancer, but I knew how to match my moves to a beat. "Work" went off and then "Come and See Me" by Party Next Door and Drake came on. It's funny because I was just saying this to Cain earlier. I started to walk off, but he pulled me back to him.

"Maybe this our song," he said, smiling, and spinning me around. We danced to at least five more songs and I finally realized we were the only ones on the floor.

"Okay, dance machine. Thanks for what you did," I said, patting Cain on the chest.

"Thanks for what?"

"You know, the pity dance." I said and giggled.

"Girl, shut your ass up. Pity? Damn, you kind of hurt my feelings," he said and shook his head.

"I didn't mean to," I said with a concerned tone.

"Damn, chill out. You need to loosen up a little bit. I was just playing. But no, it's not pity. I like you," he said before taking off running across the room.

I saw India holding her stomach and her father was holding her hand. I went to see what happened because regardless of how much I can't stand her ass, she was still my sister. When I walked over, Cain was just kneeling over her. She reached up and threw her arms around his neck, and shot me a smirk. I shook my head and laughed.

Cain ended up leaving the ballroom with her and so did her father. She is such an attention whore. I'm sure she probably saw me and Cain dancing and decided to be stupid and use the baby as a pawn. I found my friends and I looked for Marquise one more time before I just said forget it. He didn't even return the call or anything. I was starting to get pissed.

Mariah slid the room key in, and we and few other friends from school didn't waste any time pouring drinks. Natasha slid a towel in front of the door, and our friend Macy and Janay both started to twist up some weed. I kept looking at my phone and it was still nothing. I went to the bathroom and called him again, and he didn't pick up yet again; I couldn't believe him.

When I came out the bathroom, there was a knock on the door, and Natasha went and answered. She told everybody to be quiet because it might be the hotel staff. She looked through the peep hole and smiled while she opened the door.

Cain and Marquise walked in. I was pissed off at his ass too.

"I was looking for you," he said, walking up to me and kissing my cheek.

"Yeah right, I called you several times," I said and crossed my arms.

"Just come on, I gotta show you something," he said, pulling my arm.

Natasha and Mariah were both shaking their heads. Janay just looked on. I started walking, and Cain winked at me when I went past him. I felt myself melt inside.

"So, where were you?" I asked when we got on the elevator.

"If you be patient, you can see, damn." He leaned against the wall of the elevator as it took us from one floor to another.

"Well, you should have at least told me you would be gone, boy."

"Okay, damn. I'm sorry. Just chill out." He pulled me to him and kissing my forehead.

We got off and he pulled me with him down the hall until we got to the room. He turned back, smiled, and opened the door. I covered my mouth with my hand and my eyes were lit up as I looked at what he had done. There had to be a million candles lit. It made the room look beautiful as the flames illuminated the space.

"You did all this for me?" I said, surprised by his gesture.

"Why wouldn't I?" Marquise said, pulling me further into the room.

I didn't have any words, and I didn't seem to need any. He covered my mouth with his lips and started to yank at my clothes.

"Damn, you look good tonight. I swear I wanted you since I saw you downstairs," he whispered in my ear.

He pushed his hands into my underwear and I gasped at the sensation he gave me.

"Mar," I moaned.

"Yeah, baby," he said as he dropped down and pushed his head between my legs and slowly started to circle my clit with his tongue.

I found myself bouncing on his tongue until I had my orgasm and collapsed on the floor.

"Nah, get your ass up," he said, scooping me off the floor and laying me on the bed full of rose petals.

He climbed on top of me and opened my knees with his. I smiled, thinking of the first time we had sex, and him taking my virginity.

"I love you," I said as I gripped the back of his head and kissed him.

He pushed inside of me and my mouth formed an O shape from the hit my cervix took. I was in bliss until a knock on the door startled us.

"Who is that?" I asked.

Marquise looked just as confused as I was.

"I don't know, baby. Fuck that shit. You probably screaming too much." He tried to keep stroking, but the knocking didn't stop.

Marquise got up and looked through the peephole. He shook his head and got back in the bed.

"Who is it?" Something didn't feel right.

"Nobody, baby, come on."

He tried to kiss on my chest, but I wasn't about to be a damn dummy. I got up and snatched a sheet off the bed to wrapped myself in.

"Baby, come here," he said, trying to stop me.

I swung the door open and the girl who was in his face when I first got to the party was at the door. She looked surprised to see me, but she couldn't have been more surprised than I was.

"Hi, is Marquise in here? I left my purse not too long ago." She smiled like she knew was she was doing.

I almost let the tears come down my face, but I had let him do this to me again. I just shook my head and stepped aside to let the hoe in.

"Baby, I swear we ain't do shit. Tell her, Mona." He had the nerve to insult my intelligence.

"I'm a grown ass woman, I don't lie. Yes, we were just fucking in here. He ate my pussy and everything," she said with her arms folded.

"What the fuck have I done to you? Why the fuck do you keep doing this shit to me, Marquise? I swear if you ever come near me again, I will fucking kill you," I screamed. I rarely used that language, but he had pulled something out of me.

"I'm sorry, Milan! This bitch came on to me," he screamed as I ran out the room.

I was so stupid. Once a cheater, always a cheater. Natasha told me this shit would happen, and stupid me, I let it. I was wrapped in a sheet running down the stairs, not knowing where the hell I was about to go.

Once I got to the bottom, I ran out the side door, and people were looking at me like I was crazy. I took off down the street with tears coming down my cheeks, and I didn't even care. A car horn kept blowing beside me as I ran down the street looking crazy.

"Milan!" I heard Cain call out to me.

I turned to him and stopped. I was breathing so hard I felt like I was getting dizzy. He ran up to me with a jacket and threw it around me.

"What the hell are you doing out here with no clothes on? Where the fuck is Marquise?" he asked me.

I was still crying. "He back in the room with the bitch he was fucking before he took me in the same room. I'm so fucking stupid," I cried.

My head rested on his abs as I sobbed; he was that much taller than me.

"Come on, let me get you home." He picked me up and carried me to the passenger side of his car.

"Thank you, Cain," I said once we started driving.

"No problem. You can't just be running down the street naked and shit. It's some crazy mufuckas out here," he said as he eyed me.

"Yeah, I know." I continued to look out the window the whole ride to our complex.

"Oh shoot. I left my purse and everything in the room."

"Just wait at my spot for a minute, and I'ma hit my cousins up and let them know you with me."

He drove past my building and continued to the back. When we got out the car, some guys snickered as I walked by. Cain shot them a look and they shut the up. When he opened the door to his apartment I was immediately hit with cold air. He kept it freezing in there for some reason. It was like that the last few times I came over.

Let me get you a blanket." He rushed to the back and came back with a throw and a t'shirt with some shorts. I knew the clothes would be huge, but it was better than naked.

"Thank you, Cain. I'm gonna try to be gone as soon as possible. I know you gotta get ready for y'all trip tomorrow.

"Oh, you not coming now?" he asked.

"Why would I? So I can have that bastard in my face the whole time? No thank you."

"Well, my cousins and your best friend are coming, so there you go. Plus, I got my own cabin, so if you wanna kick it with me then that's cool too."

"Let me sleep on it. I was supposed to ride with his ass too. Ugh. I might just stay."

"Well ride with me. I could use the company."

"Okay," I agreed then went to take a shower.

I opened his Old Spice Fiji body wash and smelled it while I was in the shower. I bet it smelled good when he first got out the shower. What the hell was I thinking? That's my sister's baby father. I couldn't even think about him like that. Not that she wouldn't, but I'm just not her.

******

I ended up falling asleep and never made it back to my apartment. I was glad Natasha had my bag. When I woke up, I had a bag of McDonald's sitting in front of me and a coffee.

Cain was sitting in the chair fully dressed and eating.

"You had another hour to sleep. I was just getting a head start. I had to get your stuff from the hotel first, and I put it in the bedroom already so you can get dressed."

"You're so sweet, boy. I swear you like the perfect dude. Maybe too perfect." I smirked at him.

"I'm not perfect, shawty. But I'm damn close," he said in his country accent while rubbing his beard and smiling. He was a masterpiece in real life.

"I need to go get dressed huh." I got up and so did he.

"Why do you always get up when I do? I noticed that," I asked.

"Well, I guess I just got that southern hospitality shit. When a woman gets up to leave the room, you get up. Same reason I always open the door for you."

"Ohh okay," I said, biting down on my lip.

"So, why you always biting your lip, since we asking questions," he asked, getting directly in front of me.

"I don't know. I just do it when I get nervous."

"I make you nervous?"

"I don't know. I guess."

My palms started to get sweaty as he licked his lips and just looked at me. I saw him coming toward me and I accepted. We started kissing heavily. What the hell was I doing?

"I'm just gonna go get dressed," I said and walked into his bedroom.

When I turned around to close the door, he was watching me. I shook the thought of us out my head. I couldn't do that. I had finally gotten my kiss, and I was on fire.

I got dressed and cried in the room for about five minutes. I was still feeling sick about last night, and I was kind of glad I didn't have my phone so that Marquise couldn't keep feeding my lies. I fixed my face up after my crying session, and I was ready.

"Damn, I thought you fell asleep," Cain joked.

"Nah, I had some shit to get off my chest."

"You don't have to deal with shit like that, shawty. I mean, we ain't blood buddies, and shit I see enough to know you a good girl," he said as he opened the door for me.

"Thank you for that." I stood on my tippy toes to kiss his cheek.

He lifted me up and kissed my forehead. "Lil' ass," he said and carried me down the stairs.

I was cracking up because I felt so little compared to him.

"See, look at you smiling already."

Cain put me down and opened the car door for me. I slid into my seat, and he closed the door then went around and hopped in on the driver side. He was so cute, I couldn't help but look at him. He had this grin on his face like he was happy as we took off, heading toward mountain high. It was unfortunate the drive was only an hour and a half because we were having such a good time together.

Cain had made me forget why I was even sad.

Cain

I was fucked up to see her walk away to be with my cousins and her friend. That girl was special, and now I felt like I wanted her, no I needed her ass. That nigga Marquise was a fuckboy for that shit, and he just didn't know what he had. He didn't even come after shawty, and the fucked up part is Cheeky, one of our team mates said he was with the bitch Mona who fucked mostly every football player but my ass. I wasn't a saint, and I loved pussy just as much as the next nigga, but a female like Milan is hard to come by. Smart, beautiful without all that extra shit females do, and she about something.

I can't say the same for her sister. I wished I would have dismissed her at the club. I was glad I didn't get into anything too deep with her because now it would be easier for me to push up on Milan. I mean, yeah, she say she pregnant with my baby, but I ain't stupid at all. I was getting a test for sure because the way her phone was jumping whenever we were together, she wasn't just fucking me anyway, and I was sure of the shit. It was all niggas' names too, and it was funny because she thought I didn't notice the shit, but I only fucked her three times. Shit ain't bother me. I knew who was gonna be my shawty for sure. Milan didn't even know how I was about to get in her life. She was gon wanna marry a nigga. Marquise was a dumb for letting shawty slip.

I wasn't grimey, but shit, life was fair game. She was single, and so was I. I laughed at my own thoughts and went into the cabin I had chosen. It wasn't my type of spot to celebrate, but this was what everybody had voted on for some dumb ass reason. I told them Vegas was the move, but I would just have to do that shit with some of my niggas.

After I plugged my phone up in the bedroom, I turned on the TV. There was a lot of noise and shit outside, so I went to the window and saw the team already turning up. Grease, our linebacker was running toward my door; I could see him through the window. Then I heard the banging on the door.

"Come on, nigga. Get your ass out here!" he yelled and banged.

I jumped up and grabbed one of the bottles I brought with me. I came out and held up the bottle.

"Leh go!"

I came down and saw everybody already drinking and smoking. I smoked, but since I was going to this training camp, I couldn't fuck with it. Then again, the camp wasn't for another two months. I grabbed a jay from Grease and pulled hard as fuck. The music was going, and we were getting fucked up. A few girls who had tagged along kept coming up and trying to catch me faded, but I wasn't with that shit right now. I was actually looking for Milan.

In all these people, I couldn't see her ass nowhere. I looked over and saw Marquise talking to one of the cheerleaders. I shook my head. That nigga showed up and didn't even try to plead his case to his girl. Fuck it, his loss. I was feeling bold, and for some reason, I just didn't give a fuck.

I saw Milan, my cousins, and Natasha sitting on a picnic table. I walked over after cuffing Grease's blunt that he'd just rolled, and pulled Milan up off the table. I could hear all the girls saying, "Oooooh."

"What's up, Cain? I'm having a good time," she said as she danced with me. She was tipsy, and I could tell.

"You look pretty as shit, Milan," I said, drunk as shit myself.

"Thank you." She grabbed the weed and took a pull, which surprised me.

"Damn, when you start smoking?" I pressed my lips to hers to catch the smoke.

When I pulled back, she had this crazy ass smile on her face. We were talking, and she seemed to be feeling me hard as shit now. I didn't know if it was because she was drunk or whatever, but I liked her like this. She seemed to be relaxed.

"I guess I might as well turn up with everybody else." She took another pull, then pulled me to her and blew the smoke in my mouth.

"Yo, what the fuck!" Marquise walked up and said.

I shook my head and turned back to Milan. I was drunk as fuck.

"Nigga, you pushing up on my bitch?" Marquise pushed me.

This nigga must have lost his fucking mind. I pushed him back, but with my weight, his ass went flying back.

"Fuck you, nigga. You ain't know no better." I wrapped my arm around Milan and walked off.

"I knew you was a hoe!" he yelled behind us.

I turned around and took off my shirt. "Nigga, call her another hoe! You mad cuz you fucked up? She was crying and running down the street naked, and your bitch ass let her!" I said, getting in his face.

"It's cool, Cain," Milan said. "I'm the hoe? I was virgin when I let your bumpy dick ass creep in me—"

She didn't finish before Marquise slapped her across her face. I didn't even see myself throw the first punch, but I knocked his ass back. He came back, but he was no match for my hands. I laid him the fuck out with two hits. Some of our teammates came and grabbed me, but I knocked them niggas off.

"Keep that bitch, nigga, I got plenty," Marquise said while being helped up.

"I will, I'ma cuff the fuck out her too." I picked Milan up with one arm and walked to my cabin. I snatched a bottle off the table with my other arm.

"Cain," Milan said, trying to wiggle free.

"Yeah?" I said as I opened the door and walked in.

"You didn't have to do that. I don't wanna mess up nobody's friendship."

"Why the fuck would I wanna be friends with a nigga like that? He already ain't got no loyalty, so he ain't shit to me anyway."

"Cain!" Mariah ran in screaming my name.

"What the fuck you yelling for?" I asked as I poured a shot.

"Nigga, we just wanted to hi five your ass." Natasha ran up and hugged me.

"I'm glad somebody knocked that bitch ass nigga out. He calling you a hoe but got caught being one twice," Natasha said and sat next to Milan.

"I'm done with him, I swear I am," Milan said, looking like she was about to cry.

"Aight, I got her, man. Y'all go head," I said as I opened the door for them.

I saw that everybody had gone back to partying, which was good. I ain't wanna fuck up nobody's good time.

"Well, excuse us," Janay said and grabbed Mariah. They both were cheesing hard as shit.

"Y'all stop." Milan smiled as she wiped her eyes.

Janay ran up and said something in her ear, then ran out.

After they left, I sat on the bed next to Milan and pulled her to my chest.

"Why did you tell Marquise you were gonna cuff me?" she asked.

"I don't know. It sounded right to hit him back with."

"You're lying, you meant it," she said and pulled herself off my chest to look at me.

"Even if I did, we can't go there, right?" I asked.

"I wish I would have met you first, before I got with his punk ass." She crossed her leg and bit down on her lip.

I smiled and just went for it. I couldn't resist her biting her lip for shit. Pulling her on top of me, I grabbed the back of her neck and got my kiss from her ass. I couldn't stop myself, and she didn't stop me either. She was kissing me back, and her perfume smelled so good, she had a nigga's dick going strong.

I pulled her shirt over her head and showed her pretty ass titties sitting in a bra that had the periodic table of elements on it. She was straight nerd for real, but I loved that shit about her. I unhooked her bra, and her titties bounced as they dropped out. They sat up perfectly; her nipples where like caramel. I pulled one into my mouth and started to gently suck The look on Milan's face was enough to make me ready to be inside of her.

"You sure you wanna do this?" I asked.

"I know what I want, Cain." She came down and started kissing me again.

I picked her up and laid her down on the bed. She looked nervous, so I put small kisses all over her neck and chest to loosen her up.

"I'm not really the best at this, I'm just starting ou,t you could say." She slid under the covers and pulled them over her. I shook my head and snatched the blanket off.

"I ain't missing none of you, girl."

I pushed her legs back and gave her pussy a nice slow lick. He legs were shaking already. She tasted so good, I could tell she ate a lot of fruit.

"You taste like candy, shawty."

I stuck my tongue in and out her hole until I was satisfied that I was driving her crazy. I rubbed my tongue up and down her slit until she grabbed the back of my head and came in my mouth. I didn't even mind. I wanted her to sit on my face because she needed to feel some power for a minute, just so I could snatch her soul with the dick.

"Ride my face," I said as I kissed her, letting her taste her own pussy.

"I don't know how to do that stuff," she said and looked away.

"You gon' learn today."

I grabbed her up and lay down, then I pulled her right on top of my face and started slurping her tasty ass up. When Milan started to rock her hips, I could tell she was enjoying it. I started stroking my dick so I could be ready when I bust her ass wide open. As I started to feel her shake, I knew she was about to cum. I didn't even give a fuck that I didn't have a condom right now. I lifted her off my face and put her right on my dick, allowing her to slide down slowly so she could take all 11'' of it.

"Cain! Oh my God it's too big."

She moaned, which only made me want to fuck the shit out her even more. I sat up and wrapped my arms around her and dug into her pussy like I was mining for gold. She was trembling as I slow stroked her and sucked on her nipples.

"Got damn, shawty, you gon' make a nigga fall in love," I said and meant that shit.

Milan had some good ass pussy and I already knew I was about to be hooked on her ass. I started kissing her and then hit her pussy hard, so I could make her cum.

"Oh my God, it's about to happen again, Cain," she cried out as she started humping me faster until I felt her body shake.

Too bad for her, I wasn't close to being done yet. By the time I'm done with her ass, she was gonna be bow legged and in love.

India

I was so desperate to make Cain think that I'm an angel like St. Milan, that I was about to do some trifling shit. was about to do something so trifling that I didn't even believe myself.

"Okay, make sure it's my stomach and my back," I told Kitty and Channell.

"We know, damn," Channell said, catching an attitude.

"I don't think this shit is right," Kitty's stupid ass whispered.

"Just do it."

Chanel was the first one to throw a punch. After a few minutes, I started to feel sharp pains and fluids leaking between my legs. I knew Cain was on that trip, so I had to be out the hospital by the time he got back. I would pretend my phone was stolen during a robbery where I was assaulted. I fell to the ground in the alley around the corner from my house. I was in so much pain now; I felt like maybe this wasn't the best idea.

"Should we call the police?" Channell asked.

I shook my head. If they called the police, they would probably track down the caller as a witness.

"Just go!" I yelled at them.

They both took off running down the street.

"Help me!" I let out a blood curdling scream.

A few guys walked over and I was grateful as hell. I needed to get my ass to a hospital.

"You okay?" one of them ran up and said.

"I need help."

"Aye, get the bitch purse," one of them yelled.

I watched in disbelief as they snatched my purse and ran off.

"You muthafuckas!" I yelled behind them.

I saw headlights from the direction they were running in and then police lights. They took off running back toward me but they tripped over me, all three of their dumb asses. I started screaming when the police ran up.

"They stole my purse and beat me up. Help me, I'm pregnant," I cried.

They all got locked up, and the police called an ambulance to come. I knew I wasn't shit, but they wasn't shit either.

****

3 days later

I sat in the hospital and waited for my mother to come back in after talking to the doctors. I was going home tomorrow, thank God. Now I could call Cain.

"Why the hell didn't you tell me you were pregnant?" My mother walked into the room with a stern look on her face.

I hadn't called her since I came in, and the only reason I finally did was that needed a ride for tomorrow and my father didn't answer. Theirs were the only numbers I knew off the top of my head. I didn't want my mother to know at all. My father knew, though, and since my mother had no communication with my father, she wouldn't find out from him. She had stopped all contact with him after I turned 16 because she said I could make my own choices to visit him and shit.

My father blamed my mother for me being pregnant, but I convinced him it wasn't worth arguing with her about. She was always at work, so she didn't see me anyway to notice I was gaining weight in my stomach area. Hell, I didn't even notice.

"I don't know. You wouldn't have cared anyway."

"Why the hell would you think I didn't care? And I swear, if you come out the side of your neck with some shit about Milan, you gonna get slapped."

I guess all I had was the favorite card. I shrugged and looked down.

"I'm sorry, I was scared," I said in a sweet voice.

"Yeah, I bet your ass was. You lucky you didn't get yourself killed. What the hell was you doing out in the damn alley?" she asked with her hands on her hips.

"I was coming home. My car broke down at Kitty's house," I lied. My car was there, but it worked perfectly fine, more or less.

"I called your father and he on the way up here," she said.

That was unexpected. Now he's gonna know I didn't tell her.

"Oh, okay. Well, I'm tired, tell him he can come tomorrow to get me," I said and turned over.

"No, he's coming now, and I'm coming back tomorrow to get you, India. You betta produce a name for the nigga who got you up here alone." With that said, my mother left the room.

I watched TV until my father came. He asked me about Cain and why he wasn't there. I told him I didn't know his number to tell him anything since my phone was gone, and I had to hear his dumb ass speech before he left. I swear my ass couldn't wait until Cain had me living the high life. I could just imagine being a baller's wife. I fell asleep thinking about the future.

The next day, I couldn't wait to get in the house so I could go in my room and tune my mother out. She was annoying as hell, and it just seemed to never end. When we got in the house, I went straight to my room to get on Facebook. I messaged Cain and told him what happened, and waited for him to respond. It took a few minutes, but he started calling my Facebook messenger. I started to cry and then hit the answer button. He looked concerned, and I could see he was inside a car.

"Damn, you aight?" he asked.

"Yeah, are you coming back soon?" I asked, wiping the forced tears from my eyes.

"Yeah, we on the way now," he said. That *we* shit caught me.

"Oh, the team, you mean?" I asked.

He turned the camera to Milan, who was in the passenger side of his fucking car.

"Why is my sister with you?" I asked, ready to go off.

"What you mean?"

"I mean, why is my sister in my boyfriend's car?" I asked, snapping my neck.

"First of all, I can have whoever I want in my car, and second, I ain't your man, shawty. I already hipped you to that shit, man. I'ma be through to check on you."

He looked over at Milan and seemed to be telling her what happened. She took the phone from him.

"You o—"

Before she could say anything else I hung up on her ass. I was so fucking mad, I knocked everything off my nightstand.

I waited about two hours before I heard the front door open and close. I went out to the hallway and saw Cain and Milan walking in like they were a damn couple or some shit. I could see from how she smiled at him, that this bitch had fucked him. I went out and jumped into his arms and gave that bitch a smirk. Cain put me down.

"You aight?" he asked.

"What happened, India?" Milan asked with that weak ass voice.

"None of your fuckin' business, bitch. What you doin' with Cain?" I popped off on her ass.

"India!" My mother came to this bitch rescue as always.

"Ma, this is Cain. He was the baby father," I said and folded my arms.

"Well, nice of you to show up." My cut her eyes at him as she walked past.

"I didn't know until today," he explained.

"Mmmhm. Milan, I didn't know you were here, sweetie." She smiled at her and I rolled my eyes.

"Yeah, I'm just coming back from the trip I told you about," she said and cut her eyes at me.

Oh, this bitch got some balls, huh?

"So, where is Marquise?" I asked.

"None of your fucking business," Milan shot back at me.

"Milan! What the hell got into you?" my mother said.

"Sorry. Cain, you ready?" Milan asked.

I looked at him, hoping like hell he didn't leave me standing there stupid. Milan kissed our mother and walked out, with Cain right behind her. Even my mother looked confused.

"Ain't no fun when the rabbit got the gun," my mother said turned the TV on.

I rolled my eyes, went in my room, and slammed the door. Milan had me all the way fucked up.

Milan

"Cum for me, Milan," Cain demanded while he was sending me into a coma.

He was so good, I haven't been able to even think straight. I wrapped my legs around him and enjoyed every bit of him. After we enjoyed each other for what had to be hours, we laid in our own sweat and kissed like we would never see each other again. Since we got back from the mountains, we hadn't spent a day without each other. Marquise was calling and basically harassing me. After Cain confronted him about it, he finally stopped. Cain made me feel so safe.

India was on a rampage, but I really didn't care. I was tired of people thinking they can just run over me. Those days were over. Milan is going to do what the fuck she wants from now on. Besides, was what we were doing so bad? Look how India treats me, why should I owe her anything? She has done things to intentionally hurt me, and I wasn't even doing that. I just knew what felt good to me. Cain was one hell of a man, and sorry not sorry, I was taking him. Besides, even if he wasn't with me, she still wouldn't have him. He simply does not want her.

You might be wondering where my sudden boost of confidence came from. Well, when we got to the mountains, Janay pulled me into the cabin when I walked away from Cain. She told me how Cain came back to the hotel raising hell and looking for Marquise. He went to the front desk and cursed the lady out because she refused to give him the room number. She said he was pissed off, and had let it slip how much he liked me. I felt good about him, so I went with what we did. Marquise was all I knew, and I was just ready for something new. It felt so right.

"So, you coming to graduation, right?" Cain asked me as he got out the bed.

He looked like an ESPN cover. He was gorgeous. I would never have thought somebody like him would go for a plain girl like me.

"I have to. I have to write the article about graduation, remember."

I looked at my phone and saw that I had a missed call from Marshall, India's dad. He never called me out of the blue.

"Hey," I answered.

"I am so disappointed in you, Milan. I treat you like a daughter, and this is what you do?" he yelled at me.

"What did I do?" I asked, surprised at him yelling at me.

"You convinced some boys to beat my daughter up so you can have her child's father to yourself. India told me everything. After all I tried to do, and you, just like an ungrateful bitch, you bit the hand that feeds you."

I felt like I was on the verge of tears. Cain grabbed the phone and spoke into it.

"Fuck you and your hoe ass daughter's pussy. Come holla at me if you feeling some type of way." He hung up and threw my phone on the bed.

"What the fuck happened? "he asked.

"He said India told him I had some boys jump her so I can have you to myself. What the hell is wrong with her?" I screamed.

"I don't know, but fuck that shit. That nigga fuckin' with the wrong dude," he said with a different type of look on his face.

"Just forget it, Cain." I stood up and kissed him on the lips.

He was still pissed, but he started rubbing my back. "Don't trip off that shit. You know I got your ass, right?" he said and pulled me up to him.

"I know, Cain."

He kissed me. "You wanna be my girl, shawty?" he asked, catching me by surprise.

"I… I don't know. That's what you want?" I didn't know what to say. I'd never dealt with anybody like him before.

"I thought you already knew that." He cupped my face and pulled my bottom lip into his mouth.

"Be my girl," he said and kissed me again.

"Okay."

I wrapped my arms around his neck and he took me back to bed. I wasn't about to let India do this shit to me. Forget… no, fuck that bitch. Let her try me. She was about to see a new Milan.

*****

"Are you ready?" Cain called into my room again for the third time.

He was so excited for graduation. I was happy for him too. I finished my makeup and ran out, only to see him looking at his watch and shit while tapping his foot. Natasha had literally let him in like ten minutes ago, and he acted like it was more than an hour.

"I'm here, Cain, Lord," I said as I walked up and fixed his tie. I had helped him at pick out a suit at Tom Ford, and he looked sexy as hell in it too.

"You look beautiful." He kissed me on the cheek and handed me flowers. They were lilies, and they were beautiful.

"I'm not the one graduating," I reminded him.

"I can't just give you flowers because you're beautiful?" he asked.

I smiled and bit down on my bottom lip. "Girl, you know what that does to me. Don't start no shit." He kissed my neck and sent tingles everywhere.

"Come on," I said and pulled him out the door.

"I'm so proud of you," I stated.

"Thanks, shawty."

On the way to the Pavilion, we talked about what we would do if the Patriots wanted him. He would have to move, and I didn't plan to move. I was going into my final year in college and I wanted to finish at UCLA where I started. At the same time, I didn't want to lose him, and I didn't know if I was up for a long distance relationship. I guess we should have thought of that before we decided to be together.

"We can work some shit out." He kissed me and pinched my nipple. I felt it in my toes.

After he opened my door, we walked hand and hand to were the other graduates were standing.

"Go find a seat, aight, bae?" He pecked me again, and I went off to see if I could find Janay and Mariah.

I took out my phone to call them when I bumped into someone. I looked up and saw Marquise dressing in his graduation robe. I move around him, but he grabbed my arm, stopping me from walking.

"You know I still love you right."

He couldn't be serious.

"You didn't even own up to the bitch at the hotel. I'm fine, Marquise. Keep what you call love, and shove it up your ass. I should kick you in the dick for touching me right now."

"You got you a smart ass mouth all of a sudden. That nigga Cain must have your ass stupid," he said through his teeth.

"Cain definitely doing what he need to be doing to me." I put my finger in my mouth and traced it to my coochie. "And he do it all night." I bit my bottom lip and threw my head back.

"That innocent shit was an act, huh? You a hoe just like your sister. The only difference is you're worse 'cause you a sneaky hoe. Y'all are birds of a fuckin' feather, but she's better at it."

I saw Cain headed toward us and I snatched away.

"Bitch—"

"Nigga, I know I ain't see you touch my girl, mufucka!" Cain said, pulling off his robe.

"Nigga, this bitch was my pussy before you snaked in, bruh. I already said you could have her ass," Marquise said, waving Cain off.

Cain handed me his shit, but I grabbed his arm.

"Graduate, then beat his ass," I whispered to him.

He smiled and nodded. "You right." He kissed me and lifted me off the ground. I started laughing and he spun me around.

"Put me down, boy."

I kicked my legs and got down. I couldn't believe Marquise. He was acting like somebody I had never met. That little comment about India didn't go over my head either, but I wasn't going to trip. He could fuck with her if he wanted, it made me no difference. I had the prize, so she was welcome to my scraps. One thing's for sure, I was buying mace and a stun gun as soon as I could. The next time he touched me, I was gonna hurt his ass bad.

I called Mariah and told her I was there, and she led me by phone to where they were

"Wassup boo?" Janay had her arms up and hugged me as I slid past people to get to them.

"Hey y'all," I said as I sat down.

"Look at you glowing and shit. Cain must be dicking you down good," Mariah joked.

"None of your business. Y'all know Marquise just tried some bullshit outside? Cain was ready to kill him."

They looked at each other.

"That nigga better watch his self. Cain ain't his only problem if he steps to him."

"What you mean?" I asked.

The music started and they pointed toward the stage. We sat through the long ceremony until the best part came up, when they called the graduates. When they said Cain Wilson, all three of us went off. He blew a kiss at me.

"Girl, you his wife. I'm telling you," Janay said shaking me.

After the ceremony as done, we rushed to where Cain was, but he was already making his way outside. Then I thought about what I told him earlier and took off running.

"What's wrong?" Mariah called out behind me.

I was pushing through people until I made it out front. There was a group of niggas surrounding Marquise, and everybody stopped to see what was going on. I went through and saw Cain squaring up with Marquise.

"You fightin' ova a bitch, cuz?" Marquise threw a punch and missed.

Cain didn't though. He hit him right across the face, and Marquise stumbled.

"Nah nigga, don't make it about her. You bout ta know who the fuck Cain is." Cain rushed him with a barrage of blows to his body.

Marquise fell and Cain stood over him.

"This what you wanted, right?" Cain kicked him in the face then spit on him.

He turned and walked through the circle of niggas and nodded. Then the dudes started beating Marquise. I saw a woman on the phone calling the police. Cain just looked at her, and she hung the phone up. Janay and Mariah ran behind us. Cain was acting as if the shit didn't happen. He got us in the car, with Mariah driving behind us.

We all went out to eat, and didn't even talk about what happened. They all seemed un bothered. Cain didn't seem to be moved by what I would call a huge accomplishment either. It was awkward as hell for sure.

After we parted ways, Cain and I went back to his place so we could get ready to go out. He said some of his friends and their girls were having a get together in the hills. I wanted to say something about what happened, but I was too worried that he'd think I asked too many questions. I just put it out of my mind and focused on celebrating my man.

"I knew that dress would like a million dollars on you." I loved how he showered me with new clothes and stuff all the time now. He had good taste for a man.

"I love it."

It was a maxi dress with pink and black print. He also got me these pink hot ass stilettos that I had to walk in for a few days to get the hang of. Cain seemed to like me looking like this, though. He even got his cousin to hook me up with her stylist. I was now wearing my first sew in. I loved it too. I was also getting my nails and toes done now. I was changing, but I felt it was a good change.

"Look, I got my nails to match yesterday since I knew I was wearing it tonight." I said and showed him my nails.

"Look at my girl, you killing shit already."

"You always hyping me up," I said as I picked up the black silk pashmina that Cain had also bought me.

"Yup, my bitch lookin' like money," he said, standing back and rubbing his hands together.

"I don't like that phrase," I let him know.

"I wasn't trying to disrespect you. To me, it just means my girl in this instance." He corrected himself. "Let's hit this shit, and then we can go."

He pulled out a huge blunt. I still didn't smoke often, but I did with him sometimes. He lit the end and we sat on the couch pretty much snuggled up smoking. I never thought smoking could be romantic, but we looked into each other's eyes, and smoked, kissed, and even touched on each other.

"It's time, boo. Let's do the mufucka," he said and walked me out the door. We looked good!

We got to the mansion that sat right in the hills on a street called Rising Glen. I couldn't even imagine living in one of these. It was way beyond beautiful.

"Damn, can you imagine me putting you in one of these?" Cain asked, making me smile.

"Don't be getting my hopes up, Cain," I said, still taking in how nice the house was just from the outside.

"Maybe I'm not." He looked over at me as we walked to the door.

Cain went straight in like he owned it.

"My nigga Cain in this mufucka!" a dark skinned dude said as he walked up and dapped Cain. He took a pull of a Black and Mild, then stood back, looking me over.

"What up, fool?" Cain said, dapping him up.

"Who this?" the boy said, still looking at me.

"Nigga, why the fuck you staring my girl down, nigga?" Cain asked, catching an instant attitude.

"Nah, Cain, it ain't like that," the dude said, throwing his hands up in surrender.

"This Mikey, my lil brother," Cain said and pushed him.

"Nice meeting you," I said, shaking his hand.

"Oh, man. Did I tell you I saw your man? You ain't catch up with him yet, huh?" he said to Cain.

I had no idea what they were talking about.

"Not right now."

A few more dudes walked up, and I pretty much got pushed back. They were excited to see him, so I let him have his moment. I went through my phone until I saw Channell walk up. I was hoping my sister stupid ass wasn't there.

"Hey Milan," she said like we were cool or something.

"Hey," I said, still looking in my phone.

"You look cute or whatever," she said, still trying to get a conversation started.

"Thanks. What you doing here?" I asked.

"My boyfriend's cousin is here, and he invited us."

She pulled out her phone and showed me a picture. I had to look closer because I could have sworn that was the guy who ran out of India's room. His name popped up in my head from when I heard India talking to him.

"His name is Julius or Jewls, right?" I asked.

"Juelz?" she answered.

"Yeah, he was over my house with India. My mother chased him out her room," I said seriously. In reality, I was being petty as a I could be.

"You must be trippin'. Ain't no way India would do that shit," she said, getting hype.

"Oh, she wouldn't?" I asked, further planting the seed in her head.

She stormed off and I smirked. Cain walked up, and he lifted me up and started moving to Future.

"Sorry about leaving you alone." He gave me a big ass kiss.

"OOOOOOOOHHHH," I heard somebody call out. Mikey was pointing at us and laughing.

"Nigga, go get you a bitch or sum," Cain barked at him.

"Aight, nigga, damn. I just don't see you kissing on nobody. You must be pussy whipped."

"Come on, baby. This nigga…" Cain pulled me off.

I didn't like how his brother was looking at me.

"This is nice, Cain. They went all out for you." I was looking around and saw everybody watching us.

"My peoples got love for me," he said and dapped more people up.

We made it to the bar and Cain ordered us something. I didn't really hear what he said because I was looking at everybody dancing and having a good time.

"Here you go." Cain handed me a purple drink. It couldn't be anything light because I could smell the liquor.

"Thanks. So, we bout ta dance?" I asked, already moving.

"Whatever you want, baby. Finish that and we out there," he said, taking back a cup of whatever he had.

We ended up having two more drinks, then we went out and started dancing.

Doin' 80 in a 60 fuck a ticket, fuck it. Cuz I ain't had that pussy in a minute…

I was grinding up on Cain and loving how he was holding my hips and rubbing his dick against my ass. He came down in my ear and licked it.

"I swear I would go a hundred in a school zone to get to this pussy." He ran his hands over my nipples and down to my pussy.

I jumped and he started laughing. "You so nasty."

I smiled and thought about how we'd been doing it every chance we got. We stayed on the floor forever before Cain was ready to take a break.

"Let me hit the bathroom." Cain ran off, and I went back to get another drink.

I heard a loud commotion, and I saw Channell and Juelz fist fighting over in the corner. I grabbed the drink I just ordered and sipped. What the hell was wrong with me? I didn't even feel bad for starting the shit. Some people started breaking it up, and the girls pulled Channell out into the hall. Cain came back and he was looking too.

"What happened?" he asked.

"No clue. You ready to finish getting drunk?" I asked as I ordered two more drinks.

The commotion slowed down and we were still holding up the bar. I didn't even feel like dancing or nothing, I was ready to go now.

"Cain." I tapped him on the shoulder.

"Wassup, boo?"

"I'm ready," I said, almost falling over.

"Woooh, aight. Thanks for the party, y'all." Cain went around saying his goodbyes.

"See you around, Milan," Mikey said when Cain turned his back.

I didn't know what the hell he meant by that, but it didn't sound like a goodbye. It was just creepy as hell.

Cain came and grabbed me, then we left.

Channell

I was so pissed at this fucking hoe, I was going to her raggedy ass right now. I knew something was up with them because of how they act toward each whenever we were all together. I knew India wasn't shit, but I didn't think she would be that fucked up. I had something for her ass, though. I was just gonna upload it to YouTube and make some money if I go viral, but nope. I was about to expose this bitch.

I drove to her mother's house and I walked straight up and banged on the door.

"Who the fuck banging on my door like they the police?" I heard her mother yell through the door.

"Is India in there?" I said, not giving a fuck about her attitude.

"What the hell is wrong with you, chile?" She swung the door open.

"India been fuckin' my boyfriend," I said, fuming.

She raised her eyebrows. "And how you know that?" I showed her the same picture I showed Milan, and she shook her head. "Regardless, you don't come banging on my damn door like you lost your fuckin' mind. She ain't here." She slammed the iron gate and slammed the door.

I stomped off and called Kitty. She answered right away.

"Hey, Kitty, where you at?" I asked.

"I'm in the house. Why, wassup?" she said, sounding like she was smoking. That's what I needed right now.

"I'm bout ta come tell you about your girl, bitch. This bitch was fucking Juelz," I said, getting pissed all over again.

"Whooooooooooooo?" she yelled into the phone.

"Who you think, bitch? India," I said, snapping my neck like she could see me.

"Oh nah, you lying," she said in disbelief.

"I gotta get this bitch. Shit, you should be gunning for her ass too," I said, ready to bring up some old shit.

"That's not even relevant anymore," she said flatly.

India knew she liked this dude, and she ended up fucking him right there in the janitor's closet. She was such a stank bitch. Fuck both of them, but before that, I was going to show this bitch not to play with me.

"Yeah, whatever, Kitty. You think she not gonna do that shit to you again?" I asked.

"Just come on so we can smoke," she said and hung up.

I drove to Kitty's house, and when I pulled up, I saw her stepfather's car and I cringed. He was nasty looking mufucka, and he seemed to have a thing for young girls. Like a pervert.

I knocked on the door three times before somebody answered it. Kitty's mother walked off as soon as I caught the door. She went back into the kitchen, and I went straight back to Kitty's room. When I walked in, she was on her phone lying across the bed.

"Hey, girl," she said and set her phone down.

"Can you believe her, Kitty? We supposed to be fuckin' friends," I said on the verge of tears.

"I don't know what to say. I mean, fuck it. Just cut her off," she said, sitting next to me now.

"I gotta expose this bitch. Look." I showed her the video of when India was telling us to hit her. My see through phone case came in handy. I had it hung around my neck. I was happy that I was turned to her the whole time. The camera didn't catch Kitty.

"What you gonna do?" she asked.

"I'm posting it on Facebook. That's her thing, ain't it?"

I went to Facebook and uploaded the video with the caption, 'OMG'. Once it was completed, I waited for the blow up.

Kitty shook her head, then went into her drawer and pulled out some more sheets.

My notifications were already jumping. We put a towel under the door and she lit the jay she had just rolled.

"She gonna come for you, bitch," she said, shaking her head.

"Good, I don't feel like chasing her ass down."

I inhaled the smoke. She deserved worse, especially since I know whose baby that was. That's my ace right there.

*****

I had fallen asleep reading all the comments and laughing. I got 132 shares and they were still coming. India had called me several times, but I had been ignoring her. Then she started sending threatening messages, and I responded to those. I told her she could meet me anywhere. I got dressed after showering and shit, then grabbed my mace.

"I'll be right back," I told my cousin Ashley.

I jumped in my car and quickly headed to my cousins' house to pick them up. They had never liked her ass. Yeah, it might seem fucked up, this bitch had fucked with the wrong one. Once I got my cousins, Tatum, Gigi, and Meka, we headed to Brian's house. That's probably where her trifling ass would be. I had dropped her off there a few times, and of course I remembered how to get there. I got out and knocked on the door. I left my cousins in the car so it wouldn't look suspect.

"Who is it?" I heard a man yell.

"Hi, I came to see India," I said as he opened the door.

This was the nigga she was talking about she fucked. I was about to blow her whole spot up. The nigga looked me up and down, then called out for India.

She walked to the door, when she saw me, she turned her lip up.

"What's going on?" an older woman came up and asked.

"Oh, you must be Brian's mother. India been fucking your man too," I said and smiled.

India's mouth was wide open.

"What the fuck she talking about?" she said, looking at both of them.

Then, to add some topping, Brian came to the door.

"Brian, India been fucking Juelz and your stepfather here. She been putting that baby on a nigga name Cain, but it wasn't his or yours."

India must have popped because she ran at me, but I moved and she fell on her face. I heard Brian's mother cursing the dude out.

"You stupid bitch!" India got up and jumped on me.

I tried to kick her, but she caught me in the stomach. I saw my cousins run up and they grabbed her. Brian went inside and closed the door. I turned back to India fighting to get my cousins to turn her loose. I went up and punched her ass right in the nose and she started leaking. When she dropped, we all started stomping and kicking her.

I made sure to bring my knife, so I could fuck this bitch's life up. I pulled her braids up while my cousin held her down and started cutting them off and yanking them right out her scalp. My other cousins joined me in yanking her hair out.

"Opened your legs for the wrong nigga," I said, kicking her in the ribs.

She was lying on the ground in the fetal position. I didn't even have any sympathy for the bitch. We jumped in my car and peeled out.

I took out my phone and decided to make one last move. I went on Facebook and went to Milan's page.

Hey Milan. your sister was pregnant by Marquise.

Done!

Cain

Whatever Milan got in that message must have fucked with her. She'd been quiet since we'd been at the hospital. Somebody beat the shit out of India, and I guess I wouldn't be shit if I didn't go up there with Milan. I was ready to go, though. She was breathing and shit, so there was no need for me to stick around.

I had seen that Facebook video, and I couldn't believe this trifling ass bitch. I didn't give a fuck to be up there foreal off that shit alone, but Milan was so fucking forgiving, she had to be there. I didn't even confront India about the video because I didn't give a fuck about her explanation. I know she did it because the baby wasn't mine. What a trifling bitch.

I was ready to go. I had to make a play any damn way. This was supposed to be my last move, and I was happier than hell to be getting the fuck out of this shit.

My father wasn't too happy that I wasn't trying to get his crown, but he would have to just accept the shit. I want to be known for something besides pushing white and having bitches and nice whips. He was still mad about the nigga Craps, though. That nigga got ghost after that conversation with my father on the phone. I hadn't seen him since a few days before I went to the park and heard about him tryna boss up. Either my father had somebody snatch the nigga before I got to him, or he ran off because he knew he'd fucked up. He wouldn't be safe nowhere anyway, so I wasn't even worried about him.

I was getting antsy, and decided to just leave and do what I had to. Milan didn't mind me going, but she was going to stay up here with India a lot longer. India wasn't acting like her typical self, but I never believed a leopard changed spots, so I wasn't betting on her.

"Baby, let me come back and scoop you, aight?" I said and kissed her.

"Okay, call you when I'm ready," she said with a smile.

I was pissed that we got there after India's father had left. He needed to talk to me about that phone call. He still had me fucked up. I left the hospital and made my way straight to the storage unit. This one was only about ten minutes from the hospital. I pulled in like I usually did, and popped my trunk.

I put the key in the lock, and as soon as I opened it, I felt the first blow to my knee. I turned to hit whoever had just hit me, but they had already hit my ankle. I fell down as I heard footsteps running away. This shit was hurting so bad, but I had to get the key and try to make my way to my car.

Fuck!

*****

A few days later, I sat across from a doctor with Milan by my side while he told me I would never play football again. My knee was shattered and I had to get a replacement. My ankle bone was cracked, and that would take a lot of surgery to fix. I felt like a bitch because I felt my future slipping away, and all I could do was cry.

Milan laid my head on her chest and she stroked my face. The doctor left the room and Milan grabbed my face, surprising me.

"Who the fuck are you?" she asked, surprising me with her tone.

"What—"

"Who the fuck are you, nigga?" I had never heard her use that word.

"Cain," I said with a shrug.

"Oh, you must be somebody else because the Cain that hits this like he crazy don't say it like that," she said and pointed to her pussy.

"I'm fuckin' Cain," I yelled.

"That's right, and Cain don't take shit laying down. So, what you gonna do? Make your own shit happen. Yeah, you love ball, but that option is out. Now what?" she asked, looking me dead in the eyes.

"I hear you," I said, then grabbed my crutches and left the office.

My bitch was down. I done created a monster.

9 months later

"Why we pay you? To handle business! Why the fuck you calling him with this bullshit? You lucky the nice one answered," Milan said and hung the phone up on Wakeem.

He couldn't seem to keep count, and it was becoming a serious issue. Milan had basically run side by side with me in a lot of our business ventures. The past nine months were rough as hell. I was just getting off crutches, and Milan had been there with me every step. She had to start back school, but when she wasn't in class and doing homework, she was with me. She had evolved into a fucking ganstress from that quiet ass church mouse she was before. She was still sweet, and I can say it now, I loved her ass. We loved each other.

I was depressed for a little while, but I came around to finally letting go of ball. That didn't mean I couldn't dabble in it. I ended up opening a physical therapy center, and with my father's connection in the underworld, we were able to start getting celebrities and athletes. I made Milan a partner since it was actually her idea. I didn't mind breaking bread because my real business was shitting on that place, even with millions a year coming in. Oh, and Milan had that shit on lock too. She was a boss, all she needed was to have somebody bring the shit out of her.

"Babe, you need to get somebody else on that house. That fool ain't good for business," she said, sitting on my lap in my office chair.

I slid my hands over her legs, which were baby soft like every other part of her. "You know you make my dick hard when you be all bossy and shit. Where that shy shawty at?" I asked, slipping my hand into her shorts.

She bit her lip, and I knew I had to fuck her. I picked up the remote that controlled mostly everything in my office and hit the door lock button.

"Put that joint up here." I patted the desk.

Her shorts were still on, so I pulled them down and she got up on the desk. Her pussy and asshole stared back at me. She always smelled good no matter what day or time it was. I went straight for the pussy first. I put a hand on each of her ass cheeks and dove in. I loved when she ate her damn pineapples.

"You a fuckin' dessert, girl," I said with my face buried in her pussy.

My favorite part was sucking on her clit. She could never take that shit too long before she was exploding everywhere. I gave her some pussy licks, and then sucked on her clit until she was begging me. She tried to stop me, and I kept smacking her hand away. I was getting this pussy nice and ready. I knew she was about to cum because she started to move more and get excited. He sweet juices came splashing me in the face, and I held on tight, catching every drop.

"Shit, Cain," she said, trying to get down.

I pulled her off and laid her down on my desk. I stroked the tip of my dick up and down her opening while she panted in anticipation of the dick. She grabbed it and started guiding me to her pussy. She was nice and tight from that nut, so I pushed in, and the yelp I got let me know I had that pussy right. After I hit it hard a few times, it was lay the pipe time. I grabbed her shoulders and pounded her hard as shit. The faces she made were enough to make a nigga cum right now. I pulled her shirt and bra up, and went to work on those pretty ass nipples. I felt her pussy getting even more gushy and I decided I wanted to see that ass bouncing off my dick.

I pulled her down and flipped her over, then guided my dick back in. That view of her pretty ass pussy taking my dick had me hype. I lifted her leg up and started stroking her and playing with her clit. I could feel her pussy muscles tighten, and the cum came down my dick. I took my dick out to see her cumming all on the floor. Damn that shit had me ready to cum. I went back in and hit her off for another ten minutes until I was ready to cum. I pressed hard in her as I released all my seeds into her pussy.

She was laid over the desk with her legs shaking.

"Shit, I need your office to be in here whenever you start working full time," I said as I grabbed her naked ass and sat her on my lap.

"I told you I'm going to be a damn journalist, boy." She slapped my chest.

"We can own a damn station." I said and jiggled her ass.

"Whatever you say, Cain."

She picked her clothes up then went into the walk in closet I had custom built. I also had a luxury bathroom in there. My clothes were on one side, and Milan's clothes on the other. I watched her grab me and her some fresh clothes and two towels.

"Come on," she said and winked.

I got up and walked in to start on round two.

After me and Milan made a mess in the bathroom she had to go to class. I called my assistant, Lei in.

"Nice lunch, Mr Wilson?" she asked.

"Yup, I need you to send my girl some flowers and have them delivered to this classroom." I wrote down the number I copied from her schedule this morning.

"Oh, and can you get me some shrimp and broccoli? I ain't get much eating done talking to my girl," I said.

She smirked and walked out the room.

My phone was ringing, and I saw it was Mikey's simple ass. This nigga here, man. I gave him a job off muscle since that was my brother. He can't even flip a pancake. He ain't selling shit. I was going to find him a new position because he wasn't in the right business.

"What's up?" I answered.

"Bruhhh, I got that spot I was telling you about. I got this lil bitch I been fuckin' with for a few months coming to christen the joint," he yelled into the phone.

"Shit, that's wassup, nigga," I said as I fixed shit on the desk me and Milan messed up.

"Guess who the bitch is, though."

I rolled my eyes because this boy thought I gave a shit who he was fucking. He wasn't this enthusiastic when he came up short with my bread.

"Nigga, the bitch Channell from the party. The one who was fighting with Jay's cousin and shit. Yeah, I been cuffing her ass.

"Oh yeah? But anyway, I need you to start going to the cross," I said, disregarding his fool shit.

"Damn, bruh, that's the weakest spot," he complained.

"No, nigga, you the weakest link. That's where you workin' if you wanna work, nigga," I stated. I ain't had to explain shit to this nigga.

"Aight, man. But look, you think I can get a couple hundred? I need to get my car from the detailing place, and I spent all my cash," he said.

I looked at my phone and hit the end button. This nigga was bullshitting, I just paid his dumb ass a few days ago. I ain't taking care of no grown ass nigga.

****

"Hurry up," Milan whined as we walked into our newest business venture. It was a 24-hour daycare center. She was so excited to show me what she did. I know it's only been months, but this girl never ceased to amaze me. She was trying to push me to go to medical school, and it might sound dumb because I went through with school, but I just didn't have the desire to be nobody's damn doctor.

Milan hit the lights, and I was blown away. She been putting my money to good use. She had a nice lobby. It looked like some five star hotel type setup. There where iPads on stands, and I wondered what the hell that was for.

"You giving these away?" I asked.

She giggled and shook her head. "No, that's where the parents sign the kids in and out."

"Dope. So, all the classes have glass walls?" I said as I continued down the halls.

This shit was nice as fuck, it was in Beverly Hills, so she knew she had to go all out.

"I need to do some hiring too," she said, rubbing her hand across the glass.

"Why don't you run it." I asked.

"Cain, I'm not gonna keep having this conversation once again. Isn't it enough you got me in stilettos all the time and pushing dope? I'm good, okay," she said with her head leaned to the side.

I wanted her to pursue her dreams so badly, but I also wanted her to make her own money fulltime. It wasn't about the money for her, though, so I guess I should just leave the shit alone.

"Aight, shawty, come on. I'm supposed to take you shopping, remember?" I said.

"You mad?" she asked and poked her lip out.

I smiled and lifted her off the ground, bringing her eye level.

"If you happy, I'm happy, bae," I said and kissed her perfect plump lips.

"I love you, Cain."

She made my dick hard when she said my name.

"Love you too."

Mikey

FUCK CAIN! That nigga got on my fucking nerves sometimes. He really thought he was God or some shit. I loved my brother, but sometimes he did too much for me. I asked him to get a few hundred and he acted like it would break him or something. I had money, but I wanted to save it for some other shit. I looked over at Channell while she snored in my face and pushed her off the bed.

She jumped up, looking around all crazy.

"What happened?" she said as she got off the floor.

"You flipped off the bed. I tried to catch you."

"What the fuck?" she said as she got back in bed.

I fucked with her, but she was getting on my damn nerves. She thought she was that bad, that I was gonna keep her ass. I had run into her shortly after the party, and I had been fucking ever since. She had some good pussy, but it was nothing amazing. She could suck a dick like a champ, though. Thinking of that made my dick hard.

"Put your mouth to good use," I said as I pulled my dick out.

"What the fuck is that supposed to mean?"

"You know. Swallow the dick, man." I started stroking it.

She rolled her eyes and got up. "You so fuckin' disrespectful, yo. I swear I'm tired of this shit." She got up and grabbed her clothes of the floor.

I didn't give a fuck, I could call another bitch. I pulled out my phone and looked for the Milan's sister, India. Yeah, I snuck in her DM on Instagram after I stalked Milan's page and saw her. Milan was sexy as fuck, but Cain would try to kill me for that bitch, so I went for her sister's fine ass. I met her once when Cain was fucking her, and I was glad he let her go. It was my turn.

She had told me all about what happened to her and Channell, but I really didn't give a fuck about how it looked. I like India, she was a ruthless, savage bitch, and Channell was just a bitter bitch. I still liked her, though.

"Yo, you want me to come scoop you?" I asked India as Channell looked at me with hurt eyes. I tried to fuck, but she said no, so…

"I called your ass earlier," she said.

Channell came over and snatched the phone. When she looked at the screen, she smiled.

"You so stupid, boy." She laughed.

It had Mom as the contact. I smirked as she walked off and got dressed.

"Oh, let me call you back, ma," I said and hang up.

I realized I had overslept. It was already 2:00, and I was supposed to meet my family for some bullshit lunch thing my father wanted us to come to.

"Baby, did you wanna roll with me?" I asked Channell.

"For real? You're that serious about me that you want me to meet your father?" I asked.

I had told her about it yesterday, and I could tell she wanted to go.

"I am," I said, getting up and kissing her on the neck.

"I do wanna go. Can we go to my house to get some clothes?" she asked.

"Nah, I'm bout ta take you to grab a new outfit. You gotta look good," I said and jumped in the shower.

She got in with me and I finally got that throat. Damn, she sure knew how to make a nigga's toes curl. I took her to the mall, and we grabbed her some new shoes and some new clothes. I had her change in the dressing room and we gave the tag to the saleswoman. Channell was looking good as shit too. Cain ain't gonna be the only one with a bad bitch.

When we pulled up to the address my father sent, I could see Cain's new Bentley parked a few cars up. That was a nice ass car. I grabbed Channell's hand, and we went and rang the doorbell. A guy who looked like Alfred from Batman opened the door. He waved his hand and we walked into a boring ass party, from what it looked like. I didn't recognize anybody except my father and Cain.

I went over and Cain dapped me up. I hugged Milan and inhaled her perfume. She almost made my dick hard. That dress was nice and tight, and she had gotten thick as fuck too. Her shape looked perfect.

"Pops, who the fuck all these corny mufuckas?" I asked.

"These corny mufuckas is who you need to know if you wanna be anything in California, nigga. I brought you here to get your name in some pockets. I want my two sons to own this fuckin' state, and this where you start." He moved his hand in a sweeping motion.

"Oh, aight. Oh, this is Channell," I said, and pulled her up to my father.

"Nice to meet you. You ain't never had no girl meet me before. You must be special," my father said and kissed her hand.

"Nice to meet you." Channell smiled.

I snatched her back and Cain shook his head.

Milan didn't say shit the whole time we walked around. Cain seemed to be doing well talking to these old school ass niggas, but I wasn't feeling them, especially the one I was talking to right now. Your man had a greasy ass perm and some fucked up fronts. How the fuck can this nigga be a boss?

"So, hear what I tell you. You gotta make sure you got every corner locked down. There—"

"I don't need to advice on how to run shit, man. My father taught me well," I said, getting annoyed with these wanna be father type niggas.

"Who the fuck you talkin' to lil, nigga. I killed more mothafuckas than your age, and you wanna talk shit to me?" he said loud enough for everybody to hear.

"Mikey," my father called out.

"Nah, Lo. This nigga ain't got no respect," another nigga said.

I turned and saw everybody looking at me.

Cain walked up to see what was going on. "He ain't mean shit, you know how these young niggas is," my father explained.

"I can fuck with him," dude said, pointing at Cain. "This nigga ain't eating off me," he said and rubbed his hands.

My father looked at me and shook his head. We left out the house and my father pushed me.

"Nigga, your name dead out here. They don't even want you working, nigga!" He caught me across the face.

"Come on, Pop," Cain said, holding him back.

"That's why the fuck I didn't involve you at first. I knew you wasn't 'bout this life," my father had the nerve to say as he shrugged Cain off of him..

"Fuck this, take your golden boy and leave me the fuck alone then." I snatched Channell's hand.

"Golden boy? Don't get fucked up out here, Mikey," Cain said and walked up on me.

"Fuck you. nigga!" I said and pushed him.

I tried to move, but he had already connected with my jaw. I bounced back and we started fighting.

"Baby, stop," Channell cried out.

"Cut this shit out." My father tried break us up.

I let go and cracked my neck.

"Man, fuck this pussy ass nigga," Cain said, then grabbed Milan and walked off.

I walked to my car with Channell right behind me.

"What the fuck is wrong with you?" she asked, trying to keep up.

"Shut the fuck up and get the fuck in the car," I barked.

"Who the fuck you talkin' to?" she said, stopping and putting her hands on her hips.

"You, bitch, now get the fuck in the car."

"Fuck you, Mikey. You so fucking stupid sometimes," she said and walked away from me.

Channell thought I was really playing with her ass. I ran up and turned her around. She rolled her eyes and I slapped the shit out of her. Once the shock on her face was there, I slapped her ass again.

"So, I'm a bitch now?" I said, grabbing the back of her head and forcing her to look at me.

"No, baby, you ain't a bitch," she said with tears forming.

I got mad because she was the one trying to play the victim. I slapped her in the mouth then kissed her.

"Have your ass at my house when I get there. Since you wanna call yourself being smart, walk home. I swear if I see you pull up in anything, I'ma kill you and whoever is driving you."

I pushed her down and got in my car. I watched her cry on the ground then I got out and helped her up.

"If you wanna make it sooner, you can't lay here crying." I kissed her forehead and got in my car then pulled off.

I passed Cain and thought about how I would never do shit to harm my brother. I wasn't going to hurt him. I was going to take over. I called India and told her to get that pussy wet for me. By the time Channell made it to my house. I will have bust a few nuts. My dick was already hard as I drove to India's house. I wanted to fuck Channell and India both, but I knew that shit would take some time. I knocked on the door and she answered in a pair of shorts that were all up in her pussy.

"Look at you," I said, walking in and kissing her on her cute ass lips.

"You look good," she said and turned to walk off.

Her roommate was bent over the counter in a pair of shorts similar to India's. I know she was doing that shit on purpose. She wanted me to fuck her.

"Where your girl?" India asked, making fun of Channell.

She didn't mind being my side piece, and she took some personal pleasure from fucking with Channell.

"Stop talking shit about my girl, man. I'm getting serious about her," I said as I pushed my hand between her thighs from the back.

"Then why you here with me?" she asked.

"You know why."

She dropped down and started sucking my dick. It was on after that. I fucked her mouth until I felt my first nut build up. I pulled her up and started fucking her from the back. She had some good pussy, and I dove into that shit for the rest of the night. I ignored all Channell's calls. I was fucking good, and I didn't feel like driving home now. Guess she would have to walk home too since she couldn't get into my spot.

India

Yes! I had finally found a nigga who was cashing out, and it couldn't even be any better because it was Cain's brother. Oh, and to sweeten the deal, Channell's new man. I laughed out loud thinking about how she thought she was doing something by jumping me with her bull dog looking ass cousins. I had healed up and got my hair together, and now I was back. I was gonna wait to get her ass back until she thought it was sweet, and I'm already getting at her by fucking her man. Soon to be my man.

"Thanks for the money," I said and threw the stack on the dresser.

We had just finished fucking and he was lying on the bed watching TV.

"No problem, boo. You know I got you." He winked at me, and I smiled and laid back down.

"I saw your sister tonight," he said as he lit a Capone.

"So?"

"I was just saying. She fine as shit, though. You fine as mufucka too, y'all got some good ass genes."

I was starting to get irritated and was almost ready to throw his ass out.

"Well, go fuck her then," I said and grabbed my robe from the door.

"Aaaaw. You jealous?" he said, getting up and wrapping his arms around me.

"No, for what?" I rolled my eyes.

Milan really think she all that now too. That nigga Cain must got her head all hyped up and shit. He's giving that bitch what was supposed to be mine. I had to take my hat off to the bitch though, she had everybody going with that sweet girl act. She was showing out too. I hadn't seen that raggedy ass car she used to drive. Now she pushing a Porsche, and only wearing designer and shit.

I opened the door my bedroom in the 4-bedroom shared housing for UCLA. I had gotten in, and when I applied for housing, I lucked up and accidentally got placed with the upperclassmen in some system glitch.

I went to the kitchen and grabbed a bottle of water. One of my roommates was sitting on the couch watching TV. I didn't speak to these bitches and they didn't speak to me. I didn't care.

I went back to the room and I heard Mikey on the phone.

"Just wait 'til I get there then," I heard him say, then he listened to the other person. "Baby, you brought it on yourself. Don't blame me for showing you how to be a good woman to a nigga. I love you, girl."

I walked in the room and turned to him. "I gotta get up in the morning, so I think you should go home to your boo." I got under the cover and drank some water.

"I see you just jealous all together tonight, huh?"

"So, when you leaving her?" I asked and looked at him while I waited for an answer.

"I don't know, man. Why the fuck you always pressing me out about the shit?" he said as he put on his clothes."

"You right, I won't. I'ma just get me a nigga to fill the time that you don't want." I picked up the remote and started turning the channels.

"Don't make me fuck you up, India." He put on his shoes and fastened his belt.

"So, you can have a whole bitch, and you want me to just play side chick? Nah. You know what, this shit ain't gonna work for me," I said and got up.

"Bitch, sit your ass down. I will see you in a few days."

He kissed me on the cheek and walked out. He must have been a fool. I told Brian to come over right after I heard his car start up and pull off. Brian didn't believe shit Channell said. I had him so pussy whipped that I convinced him that she was jealous of us. But right now, I was more than surprised that he didn't answer me. He must be asleep. I lay down and just went to bed, another lonely ass night. I tossed and turned until I fell asleep.

*****

"Come your lazy ass on, India!" my mother yelled to me while I sat in my old bedroom. She wanted me to help her set up for the party. She was throwing a party for a bunch of Geritol smelling old heads. The food was a good reason to be there, though. I had invited Brian, who I had cursed out thoroughly for not answering the phone last night.

"I'm coming!" I yelled back.

As I walked to the door, I saw my old cheerleader trophies and decided I would try to join the school's cheerleading squad. When I walked out, my mother was dancing around the living room. She draped a streamer around my neck while she moved to Frankie Beverly and Maze. I laughed and danced with her. This was the first time in a long time that we'd shared a nice moment.

"You look pretty with your hair like that." My mother pushed a piece of my bang out of my face. She covered her hands with her mouth. "Oh my God, I meant to give you this, this morning. I had to wait until I got paid again, but here you go. She went and grabbed an envelope from the china cabinet drawer. I opened it, and it was a card stuffed with money.

"I'm so proud of you, India. I've been saving two hundred dollars a month since you were a year old. I knew you would go to college and need it. I love you, sweetie." She kissed me on the cheek and hugged me.

I started crying because I never thought she cared that much to do something like this for me.

"Thank you, Ma." I hugged her tighter.

"You're my baby girl, I love you, and don't ever forget that." She wiped my tears and I helped her put the streamers up.

After the party started, I sat in the corner eating cake while talking to Brian. I felt like something was off with him. Maybe he had grown tired of me. Oh well, we all gotta more on sometimes.

I looked over at the door and saw Milan and that bitch Natasha walk in. I was already drunk and I took down another cup. She smiled at me and I walked over to speak. Or whatever you wanna call it.

Milan

My mother refused to hang up until I got to her house. She wanted to make sure I was coming this time for sure. Natasha had come with me to help me get through this whack ass night. My mother was having a cookout for her coworkers, and it was nothing but a bunch of catty ass irritating broads.

"So, honey, I'm loving this new Milan. I ain't never seen a bitch so fly every day for no reason. Yes, I'm jealous and need to borrow some of them new shoes Cain loaded you up with." She pointed to my new Gianvito Ross ankle boots.

"I told Cain they cost too much, but he said he wouldn't have me wearing cheap shit. They cost $1100 dollars and he did it like it wasn't nothing.

"You can borrow anytime, and you know it," I said and smiled at her.

"No, for real though, sis. You changing, and I love it. He got you lookin' cute, stay with money. Bitch you hit the jackpot," she said with her tongue out.

"He one hell of a dude. I never met anybody like him." I smiled, thinking about Cain. He was slowly changing my world.

"Well, I'm happy for you, boo," she said while scrolling through her phone.

"Ugh, here we go," I said as I passed mom's house.

There were cars everywhere, and I had to park two blocks down. I went in the side door and pulled out one of the blunts Cain had rolled for me. I had picked up a habit of smoking. I wasn't bad, though, it was every now and again.

"Yes, spark it up." Natasha clapped.

We smoked as we walked down the street to the house. I popped some gum in my mouth and put Visine in my eyes to get rid of the red. We walked in and immediately started laughing. Some of them dressed like they were in the 70's and couldn't get to the new millennium.

"Milan, stop." Natasha laughed in my ear.

My mother walked toward us and we tried to straighten up.

"Hey, Milan," she said and kissed me on the cheek.

"Hey," I said pulling back.

"Ms. Natasha. You get cuter every time I see you, chile." They hugged.

India was sitting over on the couch with that low life she's always with. She got up and came over.

"Hey, big sis," she said with her arms folded.

I knew she was ready to start some shit.

"Hey, India," I said and walked past her.

"Oh, she's been getting dick from Cain now. She too good to talk to her lil sis, huh?" she slurred.

"Bitch, don't worry about my nigga's dick. You worry about that nigga and how ever many other dudes you open them legs for," I said and pointed at Brian.

"Are y'all crazy arguing in the middle of my party?" My mother came up on us.

"She started it," I said, ready to knock her ass out.

"You still mad over dick, India? Let it go."

"You wild as shit shorty," Brian said, getting up. "You fighting her over a nigga in my fuckin' face?" He got up and left out. India ran behind him.

"What the hell has gotten into you? You all painted up and dressed like one of these fake ass bad and bougee bitches," my mother yelled at me.

"Are you serious? You know how she is."

"Whatever, bye Milan," she said and pointed to the door.

I was crushed because for the first time I felt like I let my mother down. "Really Momma? She has treated me like dirt for all these years and I took it. Now that I've finally stood up for myself, you turn on me?"

"Milan, don't ever say that. You know that I would never turn on you. I am your mother and I love you, but I'm her mother too, and I love her just the same. You two are sisters. One day I won't be here, and you'll only have each other. I just don't want my children to fight. Is that so bad?" she said with tears in her eyes.

"Then tell that bitch that," I uttered as I walked out the door.

India was standing in the front wrapping her hair up.

"Bitch, you swear you something special. You tried to play me in front of my nigga!" she screamed, coming toward me.

I don't know what came over me, but I reared back and punched her dead in the nose, then I kept going until I was over top of her beating on her all over her body. Natasha pulled me off.

"Yeah, talk now, India. You swore you could beat me for years, see me now!"

"I ain't finished," India said, getting up and trying to fix herself up.

"Yeah, you are!" Natasha said to her as she pulled me off. As we walked to the car, I never felt so pissed.

"You finally whopped her ass." Natasha laughed.

I couldn't help but to smirk. I gave her my keys and let her drive. When we got home, I saw Cain sitting in the parking lot. I got out and knocked on his window.

"What's up?" I asked. He didn't tell me he was coming by.

"My father had a heart attack," he said and ran his hand over his hair.

"Oh my God.

"Get in," he demanded.

I waved to Natasha and got in. He backed out and zoomed off.

"Is he okay?" I asked.

"He's in the emergency room. That's where we headed.

"Okay." I didn't want to press him out.

When we got to the hospital, Mikey was sitting there with Channell.

"Wassup," he said to us.

"How he doing?" Cain asked.

"He's stable now. They said we can't see him yet, though.

"Aight."

We sat down and waited a while. Cain held my hand the whole time, and I could feel how tense he was. They came in after a while and told us to come back tomorrow. Cain almost went crazy, but I calmed him down.

****

"Thank you for being there for me, baby," Cain said.

"Why wouldn't I be?" I asked.

"I don't know, I never had a broad this involved in my life."

"I hope that's a good thing."

"It is." He pulled out a long red velvet box.

"Baby, you need to stop buying me all this stuff," I said as I looked into the box and pulled out a beautiful locket with our picture in it.

"You like?" he asked as he kissed my neck.

"Of course I do, Cain. Thank you." I as he kissed down my stomach.

"You sure you wanna do this?" I asked. He'd just found out about his father. I wanted him to be okay before he thought about pussy.

"Shhhhh. This my pussy, right?" he said as he pulled my pants off.

"It's yours." I moaned as he kissed my thighs.

"Yeah, I know," he said and slid into me.

"Shit, Milan. I gotta cum in you, shawty."

"What? No, you gonna get me pregnant." I tried to be serious while he was giving me what he called death strokes. I was clawing at his back while he dug deep inside of me.

"Cain." I screamed right before I came.

He pushed inside me and left it there. I could feel his veins pulsating.

"Did you just cum in me, Cain?" I smacked him on the arm.

"I told you I was, though." He kissed me and shoved his tongue into my mouth.

"I hope the baby look just like you, ma."

He kissed my neck and I ran to the bathroom to squeeze it out.

"I can't believe you." I was so mad at him.

"Aaaw, you just think if you get fat I won't want you. I swear, even if I saw you shoving a whole cheesecake in your mouth, I'ma still be like, that's bae." He smiled and wrapped his arm around me from the back, making me face the bathroom mirror.

"I'm not ready for a baby," I said honestly.

"I know, I'm sorry. I just knew I had to cum in you. The shit was feeling too good already." He laughed and smacked my butt.

I couldn't go through another abortion, so I was going to make sure to get a plan B.

2 weeks later

I was so glad we left Cain's father's house. We were checking up on him and making sure he was doing good. Mikey was there and acting just as much of a bitch as he always does. I didn't care for that idiot at all. He wasn't good for shit but running his mouth. I couldn't stand his ass. Cain's ass was pissed off the whole night. I didn't like to be around him when he was mad because he would be snappy and shit. He tried to be soft with me, but it would always come out.

"Baby, you can drop me off at home," I said, referring to my apartment with Natasha.

I didn't have the heart to move out, so I stayed to help her with bills. We were still tight, but she had a man now, and she was always running out. She also didn't hide the fact she thought I was fucking up by getting mixed up in Cain's world, but she liked him for me. I let her know I was a grown woman and could make my own decisions. You might also think I'm stupid, but I think I'm smart. I'm building shit with Cain. I didn't want to do too much because it wasn't like we were married or even close, but I just fell hard for the dude, and he changed how I thought about shit.

I don't take shit from anybody anymore because Cain showed me I could do better. Yeah, my mouth got a lil dirty, but shit, people change. I don't really talk to India much, but she didn't play with me like she used too. She was still a bitch, but she didn't come at me sideways no more. I had started to carry a gun and everything. Cain told me you could never get caught slipping, and that's what I was making sure of.

"You ain't tryna stay with me?" he asked.

"Not if you in one of your angry spells."

"I'm sorry, bae, that nigga just gotta way of makin' you wanna beat his ass," he said as he rubbed his neck.

"I can tell. You wanna spend the night?" I asked.

"That's cool. But for real, you need to stop fronting and move in with a nigga."

"Nope. I can't leave Tash hanging." I said.

"You won't be. I would pay her rent for a year if you just stay with me."

Why buy the cow when you can have the milk for free?" I teased.

"You know you my wife, stop playing."

I flipped my hand back and forth, looking for a ring. "I don't see no rings on my finger, nigga," I said with a smirk.

"Oh, you want a ring?" he asked and fake punched me in the eye.

I swatted his hand and laughed. "I ain't ready for no ring anyway, boy."

"All women want a ring, shawty," he said as he pulled into our complex.

"Aww, you miss the complex?" I asked. Cain had moved into a nice house in the hills.

"I miss you living close."

"Oh, hush. Come on." I opened the door and he pulled me back.

"You don't open no doors."

He got out and walked around to open my door. I got out and we headed into the building.

When we walked in, it was pitch black inside. I could hear the TV on in Natasha room. We went straight to my room and got dressed in pajamas. I grabbed the money order, slid it under Natasha's door, and knocked. I went in the room to lay down and Cain was already watching TV. I smiled and climbed on top of him.

"I don't care how mad you are, nigga, you gonna get this werk." I laughed and pulled his dick out. I couldn't wait.

****

The next morning, I woke up to bacon cooking. I could smell it and started to get hungry thinking about how good it smelled. I saw that Cain wasn't in the bed, so I went out and saw him in the kitchen. I went to Natasha's door and noticed that the end of the money order was still there. I knocked and turned the knob. The door was already unlocked. I walked in and screamed to the top of my lungs.

Natasha was naked with blood all over her thighs and a pool of blood around her head.

To be continued

CPSIA information can be obtained
at www.ICGtesting.com
Printed in the USA
LVHW032357011019
632928LV00005B/190/P